MW01104075

HAUNTED

Also by Barbara Haworth-Attard

A Is for Angst
Forget–Me–Not
Theories of Relativity
Dear Canada: A Trail of Broken Dreams
Irish Chain
Flying Geese
Love–Lies–Bleeding
Wynd Magic
Buried Treasure
Home Child
Truth Singer
The Three Wishbells
Dark of the Moon

BARBARA HAWORTH-ATTARD

HAUNTED

Harper*Trophy*Canada™
An imprint of HarperCollins*PublishersLtd*

Haunted

Copyright © 2009 by Barbara Haworth-Attard.
All rights reserved.

Published by Harper*Trophy*Canada™,
an imprint of HarperCollins Publishers Ltd.

No part of this book may be used or reproduced in any
manner whatsoever without prior written permission,
except in the case of brief quotations
embodied in reviews.

Harper*Trophy*Canada™ is a trademark of HarperCollins Publishers.

First Edition

HarperCollins books may be purchased for educational,
business, or sales promotional use through
our Special Markets Department.

HarperCollins Publishers Ltd
2 Bloor Street East, 20th Floor
Toronto, Ontario, Canada
M4W 1A8

www.harpercollins.ca

Library and Archives Canada Cataloguing in Publication

Haworth-Attard, Barbara, 1953–
    Haunted / Barbara Haworth-Attard.

ISBN 978-0-00-200821-1

    I. Title.
PS8565.A865H38 2009   jC813'.54   C2009-903461-1

9 8 7 6 5 4 3 2 1

In loving memory of Ron Hibbert.
I miss you every day.

CHAPTER ONE

Dee spread feed over the ground, calling, "chick, chick." A commotion on the dirt road in front of her brown clapboard house—men's shouts, and the rumble of automobiles—brought her head up. The stiff, black helmets of Chief O'Brien and Constable Carter bobbed past the wooden fence that kept Trojan, the pig, at home. Various other hats followed. Something big was going on.

With a wide sweep of her arm, Dee emptied her pan of corn and ran for the front gate, anxious to see what had the air fairly crackling with excitement.

Gran's voice called her back. "Pull a few of those weeds from around the cabbages," she ordered.

Dee groaned. "Those weeds need pulling like I need a hole in my head," she confided to Trojan as she rounded the house to the back kitchen garden. Nobody pulled weeds in October, as all but the hardiest vegetables were long gone. Gran just wanted her to "keep out of it."

"There's no point in going out looking for trouble. It will

find you soon enough," Gran always said. In fact, now that Dee thought about it, Gran had a sour saying for just about anything that was fun or exciting.

So Dee tugged weeds, and fumed and speculated about the fracas outside the gate. She had just decided that a hunter had shot his leg off up the mountain when Gran came out on the back porch with Dee's bookbag and lunch pail.

"Off you go, now. Straight to school and straight home after."

Dee didn't need any extra urging to leave for school today. She was dying to find out what the commotion was, and for sure, Billy Haynes would know.

Gran and Dee's small house was the last before the mountain. In fact, Price's Corners Road ended a quarter of a mile past their laneway, where it split in two, becoming Mountain View Road to the right and Pike Road to the left. If a person insisted on travelling straight ahead, he or she would find a narrow, weed-lined path that led to a small wooden footbridge straddling Dickson Creek. On the other side of the bridge, the well-worn path wandered up the mountain. But Dee turned her back to all of that because the schoolhouse was a mile and a half back down the road, in Price's Corners.

The village was aptly named, as it was situated where two roads, Price's Corners Road and the Wallen town road, crossed, creating four corners. On each of these stood a building: the yellow-brick schoolhouse; Simpsons' Mercantile, distinctive for being two storeys with living quarters above the store for Mr. and Mrs. Simpson; the stately Christ Anglican church; and the stone police house. Clustered around these main buildings were smaller houses and a few businesses, such as the livery. These spread down the roads in all four directions, eventually thinning to give way to sporadic farms.

Billy Haynes lived on one of these farms, half a mile down the dirt road from Dee. They walked to school together every day and had been doing so since Dee was five. But this would be the last year. Dee's secret hope, not yet shared with her grandmother, was to board in Wallen, ten miles away, and go to the high school there when she turned fifteen next year. Billy's school days would end and he would work in the fields with his father.

When Dee got to her gate, Billy was already running up the road, fit to burst with news. He abruptly slowed to a walk when he saw her. Dee swallowed a grin. Over the summer Billy's voice had changed, fieldwork had broadened his shoulders, and he had shot up a good foot in height. He tried to talk more slowly and act calm like his dad, wanting to be seen as a grown man. But today, eagerness got the better of him, and his voice cracked into a higher pitch as his words tumbled out.

"They found a body on Pike's Mountain, well, bones. They found bones." He pointed to the automobiles parked at the side of the road. "They've gone up to see them. Dad's gone with them to show the way. He was the one who found them.

The bones, I mean," Billy added proudly. "We'll probably have the police come to our house. And maybe it will be in the newspaper," he went on.

"Probably just a hunter who shot himself, or maybe even a deer your dad thought was a person," Dee said, her nose suddenly out of joint. It was true that she had wanted to know what was going on, but now that she knew, she wished it was her and not Billy who knew everything. The fun was in telling the story first-hand, rather than hearing it second-hand.

Billy ignored her bitter tone and continued to talk non-stop about the bones and how his dad had been hunting and found them and how Chief O'Brien had asked for his dad in particular to lead them because his dad knew the mountain like the back of his hand.

"Not better than Podge, though. Podge knows it best," Dee interrupted, still feeling grumpy. She turned and walked backwards, staring up at the mountain. Morning mist blotted out the blaze of yellowed oaks and reddened maples on the lower slopes, though crimson patches appeared here and there where the sun's warm rays had poked holes in the white curtain.

Pike's Mountain wasn't really a mountain; people thereabouts just called it that. In fact, most folks on seeing it for the first time were disappointed to find that Pike's Mountain was merely a higher section of a large stone spine that snaked through Ontario. Miss Hamilton, their teacher, told them that this "spine" was called an escarpment and that it stretched from

Lake Ontario, north past Price's Corners to Georgian Bay, where it turned and dipped into the United States.

Once people got over their disappointment of the mountain not really being a mountain, they would ask how it got its name. That question always surprised Dee. Pike's Mountain got its name from the first people who settled in the area in the 1780s, the Pikes. Just like Henderson Ridge got its name from the Henderson family, and Dickson Creek from the Dicksons. Family was also the reason the nearby town was called Wallen, and why her village was called Price's Corners. That was the way it worked. The families with the most dead in the churchyard got to have their name attached to a town, a road, a stream or a mountain. Gran had lived a long time in Price's Corners—since she was a young girl named MacLeod, before she became a Vale—but neither she nor Dee's grandfather had lived there long enough to have their names attached to anything.

Once people had the name sorted out, they admitted that the mountain was quite pretty, even beautiful, and Dee couldn't help but agree. She loved everything about the mountain: the summer storms that boiled black and came roaring down to flood their yard and set the chickens squawking. In winter, stinging snow slanted sideways and fell so dense, a person couldn't even tell a mountain was there—until the sun came out and turned the slopes into diamond shards so bright, your eyes watered. In late autumn, the lower slopes exploded in colour. In all seasons, the mountain was Dee's playground.

She and Billy, along with her best friend, Clooey, and the other village children, played on every single bit of it. They built forts, had been pirates, gangsters, and soldiers; had shivered in the cold spring-fed streams and dipped under the waterfalls on hot days. Mostly, though, they played in the clearing half-way up the mountain. It was a pretty place, ringed by trees that gave a sense of guardianship. Within this circle, the grass grew long and luxuriant, soft to lie on, with few of the stinging burrs and nettles that plagued the rest of the mountain. Except there had been little time for playing the last two years. Gran had kept Dee close to home, busy with chores, telling her she was too old to be running wild. Dee had been upset at first, then discovered it was the same for everyone else. Billy had to work on the farm, and Clooey was needed by her mother to help with her younger brothers and sisters.

Her mind turned again to the bones. With all those sea-sons of exploring the mountain, it was inevitable that the children would find some sort of bones. Animals' mostly, but one time they had found a human skeleton, unearthed by a heavy rainstorm. Clooey had nearly fainted on the spot at the sight of the eyeless skull, but Dee had pretended she wasn't scared because of Billy. There would be no end of teasing from him if he saw her shrieking and carrying on. Instead, she'd swal-lowed hard and ran down the mountain to summon Chief O'Brien, who had been Constable O'Brien at that time. The bones were examined by Dr. Hughes, who later told them that the skeleton was a hundred years old, belonging to a vagabond or settler who had fallen ill or got lost on the mountain. The bones were given a decent burial in the churchyard.

"Probably just an old pioneer like last time," Dee said, though more to herself than to Billy, because she needed reassurance, needed the reassurance because a *feeling* grew inside her.

Gran told her she wasn't to pay any mind to her *feelings*—they were just that—feelings and nothing else, but after living with her particular *feelings* all her life, Dee knew better. There were feelings and then there were *feelings*. Like now: a tightening in her chest, a slight tremor in her hands, and dread churning in her stomach, leaving her queasy. It was hard not to pay *that* any mind.

As Dee stared at the mountain, a black cloud suddenly formed halfway up, spreading and oozing down the tree-clad slopes. She inhaled sharply.

"What?" Billy asked. He turned back to look, but it was gone, as quickly as it had appeared.

"Nothing," Dee said. She whirled about, eyes on the dirt road and on the grey puffs of dust raised by her boots, trying to forget the dark cloud, the bones.

It didn't work. Those bones—they'd worked their way right inside her, nagging, asking to be noticed. Why had the bones surfaced now? It wasn't rain that had revealed them; the ground was hard-packed from three weeks of unrelenting sun. Animals? Were there bite marks on them from sharp teeth?

Was a leg or arm missing, or dragged away? Or were they laid out, quiet and undisturbed beneath layers of browned pine needles? She wouldn't mind being laid out that way herself when her time came. Preferable to Reverend McAllister and the churchyard anyway.

Did fragments of flesh cling to them, like the turkey leavings after Thanksgiving dinner? Was a lock of hair still sprouting from the skull? Or were the bones old and brittle, crumbling to dust when touched?

"Dee?" Billy said. "Dee? Did you hear me?"

"What?"

"I said that Chief O'Brien couldn't find Dr. Hughes to take with them up the mountain. They can't move the bones until the doctor sees them. I shouldn't have told you about the bones," Billy said. "Ma says girls are squeamish."

"There's nothing squeamish about me," Dee said firmly. And there wasn't. Helping Gran with her midwifery the last couple of years, she'd seen more awful sights than most girls her age, and she'd never once swooned.

They came to the Holmes house, grey and worn, the gate hanging crookedly on one hinge. Podge stood waiting behind it, like he did every day. Seeing them, he lumbered out, grinning widely, shirt buttoned askew over his fat belly, a bag with his whittling in one large hand and a lunch pail of porridge swinging from the other. Baptized George Thomas Holmes, Podge got his nickname because of his love of porridge. Every day he went to the schoolhouse with Billy and Dee, except he wasn't allowed inside because he was too old and too dumb for education. "There is no place for the feeble-minded in a school," was what their teacher, Miss Hamilton, had said.

Dee suspected that Podge's large man's body with a flat moon face, bulging eyes, and young child's mind scared the teacher. He was Mrs. Holmes's only child. Mr. Holmes, unable to bear the sight of his idiot son, left when Podge was two. With no man in the house, Mrs. Holmes took in laundry from the mill workers to make ends meet. She loved Podge fiercely.

Every day Podge sat in the school's play yard, scratching in the dirt or whittling wooden animal figures until noon-time, when he'd eat his porridge and play with the children. Then he'd wait again all afternoon to walk home from school with Billy and Dee. He was happy, and Podge's mother was happy to have him out from underfoot. Dee didn't understand why Miss Hamilton was scared of him. Everyone knew Podge was harmless.

"Maybe you just don't know you're squeamish because you're a girl, and it would stand to reason that you wouldn't know you were more squeamish than a boy because you're not a boy."

Dee stared at Billy in disgust. "That's just plain stupid. That's almost more stupid than anything Podge would say, and everyone knows Podge was born simple."

"I was born stupid," Podge agreed happily.

Dee didn't feel bad calling Podge stupid. Podge being stupid was like her, Dee, having curly brown hair and light green eyes. It just was. Dee did, though, occasionally wonder what the inside of Podge's head looked like. Was there a brain in there, or was it just empty space between his ears? Was that why he couldn't add numbers or spell words? But he could whittle. From a piece of wood Podge could carve a squirrel or bird as lifelike as any she'd seen.

"Podge is what can happen when first cousins marry or when the mother is too old for child-bearing," Gran had said. And she should know. Gran had delivered most of the children, and their parents, in and around Price's Corners. It was odd, Dee thought, that Gran, who had delivered so many children, had herself birthed only two: a boy, who died when barely a week old and was buried in the churchyard with Grandpa Vale, and Dee's mother, alive, but her whereabouts unknown.

Gran had been the main birth help for mothers in the area until sixteen years ago, when Dr. Hughes arrived in nearby Wallen, a young man recently married and with new ideas. For a while, people wanted the new doctor to deliver their babies, though that meant they sometimes had to go to the hospital in Wallen. That novelty soon lost its sheen. First, there was the long distance to travel to get to Wallen, and when they got there, the doctor wanted cash to deliver the babies. People soon discovered that they were just as happy to have their babies born in their own homes, and to pay Gran with fresh-caught fish or fruit or vegetables when cash was scarce. But still, the arrival of the doctor left Gran with fewer babies to deliver.

Then the war came, and in 1915 Dr. Hughes left to be an army doctor. For four years Gran was busy again, and before long Dee was old enough to help. But five months ago Dr. Hughes had returned from overseas. The general opinion now was that a qualified doctor who knew about new medicines, such as Aspirin, was a better choice than a midwife with her homemade remedies. There were, though, a few who preferred Dee's grandmother.

And Dr. Hughes, he might disapprove of Gran's activities, but the truth was, he didn't want to be travelling all over the countryside at the inconvenient times that most babies chose to be born. He also knew there wasn't much about birthing that Gran didn't know—knowledge that she tried to teach her granddaughter, Dee.

But Dee didn't want to be a midwife. She'd decided it was just a way for Gran to keep her in Price's Corners. She'd also decided that Gran had done the same thing to Mama, tried to keep her daughter in the small village, and Mama, well, she'd had enough of Gran and her sour ways and had left, though it also meant leaving her newborn baby.

"Do you want me to carry your school books?" Billy asked, ignoring Dee's insults.

"Why?" Dee said.

"Ma says girls like having their books carried by boys."

"I'll carry your books, Dee," Podge said.

He grabbed Dee's bookbag and managed to send both his own and hers flying into the ditch. He stood looking at them, unsure which bag to go for first. Finally, Dee picked up hers, and then Podge's.

"Now see what you've done?" Dee said to Billy. She brushed dust off her bag. "I can carry my books just fine myself."

What on earth had got into him? Puzzling over Billy's behaviour almost put the bones right out of her mind. Almost, but not quite, for they had arrived at the yellow-brick school-house, and there was Clooey waiting for her in front of the school swing like she did every morning. Clooey lived in the opposite direction from the school as Dee, and she wouldn't yet know about the morning's goings-on up the mountain.

Dee broke into a run to reach Clooey before Billy. "Clooey, did you hear about the bones?" she said hurriedly. "They found them up on the mountain. People bones."

Clooey squealed, and her grey eyes widened fearfully. Dee felt a surge of satisfaction. Clooey never disappointed.

CHAPTER TWO

Disappointment. Dee's mama had disappointed Gran, and Dee believed that she, too, was fated to disappoint her grandmother. Her mama's final disappointment before slipping away in the night, leaving Gran and the newborn, was to bestow the name Defiance on her daughter. Most folks called the baby and then the girl "Dee," but Gran, after so many disappointments, couldn't swallow this one and called her "Granddaughter." At least that is what Dee believed, and her grandmother had never indicated otherwise. Dee also believed that all these disappointments were stored in the deep grooves on either side of her grandmother's mouth, a mouth that seldom smiled.

Whenever Dee felt a hunger to hear her full name, she would stop at Cissy Price's place. Cissy had been her mama's best friend. Gran might not want to discuss Dee's mother, but Cissy always had a funny story to tell about Mama. Only two other people used her full name: Miss Hamilton, when Dee hadn't done her homework, and Reverend McAllister. The minister seemed to savour her name, rolling it around in his mouth, tasting its wickedness; wicked because everyone knew Dee didn't have a father. Another of Gran's disappointments.

"Dee-fi-ance!" This morning Miss Hamilton drew out Dee's name, making every syllable ring with displeasure.

Everyone in the classroom, from the smallest to the biggest, looked up, expectant. Someone was going to get into trouble. Clooey, Dee's seatmate, reached under the desk and gave Dee's hand a sympathetic squeeze.

Miss Hamilton noisily shuffled papers on her desk. "I don't see your essay on Mr. William Shakespeare's *Hamlet.*"

"I didn't have time to do it, Miss Hamilton," Dee began.

"Stand up when you speak to me."

Dee got up from her seat. "Sorry, Miss Hamilton. I had to go with Gran to a birth last night," she explained. "We didn't get back until late."

"And there was no time this morning to work on it?" Miss Hamilton asked.

"Chores—Miss," she added quickly.

She tried not to let her annoyance show, but Miss Hamilton should know that every girl and boy in the school had chores to do in the morning. In fact, the older boys had so many chores they didn't start classes until November—not that there were many of them, as few of the boys at the school were older than thirteen. The only reason Billy got to go to school until he was fourteen was because his mother had put her foot down and insisted that Billy, the only boy of seven children, get as much education as he could. Mrs. Haynes was very big on education, and Billy's dad thought it more prudent to give in to his wife on this point than to endure a life of cold silence.

"You can't neglect your homework," Miss Hamilton said, but without much conviction. Parents' wishes came before teachers'. "It's Tuesday, so I'll expect your essay by the end of the week. That should give you time to work on it. You will be automatically deducted ten marks for lateness, so please pay attention to the quality of your writing."

"Yes, Miss." Dee sat down. It was more than she had expected. Still, she'd have to work hard to make up those ten marks. She needed good grades to pass her high school entrance exams.

A wad of paper struck Dee in the back of the neck. She placed her hand over the sting as she whirled her head around to glare at Billy. He grinned and flicked another paper ball at her. Dee ignored him and turned back around in her seat.

"Grades one, two, and three can practise their penmanship. Grades four and five, I have mathematics questions on the blackboard for you. Please work on them quietly. Grades six, seven, and eight, we will have a geography lesson."

The smaller children pulled out their notebooks and bent their heads to their work. City schools were large, with a classroom for each grade, but here in the village, all the students from grade one through to grade eight were taught together.

They sat in rows at their wooden desks, youngest at the front, oldest at the back.

Miss Hamilton stepped to the far side of the blackboard and pulled down the rolled-up world map, tapping her wooden pointer on a long, squirming line of brown inverted Vs that ran through the pink province of British Columbia. "These, class, are the Rocky Mountains." She turned and smiled at the students. "I know we have our own mountain . . ."

Dee was outraged. Miss Hamilton wasn't even from around here. She had no right to call the mountain *hers*. She came from Toronto to Price's Corners, as grateful for a job as anyone was these days, and no matter the pay, so long as she got enough to eat. Dee glanced behind her at Billy. He mouthed, "Our mountain?" And Dee instantly forgave him for knowing about the bones first, and wanting to carry her books, and flicking paper balls at her.

But Miss Hamilton and her talk of mountains had brought back all of Dee's uneasiness. Even when she resolutely set her mind to her school work, Dee found her eyes wandering to the window and Pike's Mountain.

Dee turned into Cissy Price's, leaving Podge and Billy to continue home on their own. She felt the need for a bit of kindness. Cissy, with her gentle face and kind smile, was the one who told Dee she was pretty, who wrapped an arm around her when she needed comforting, and gave her the gift of her name, Defiance. Gran was—well, Gran. She took care of Dee's needs, like food and shelter, but Cissy was more like what Dee thought a mother would be.

Cissy lived in a rambling red-brick house on the outskirts of the village, a home passed down, and added on to, through the ranks of the Price family. Numerous ginger-haired children ran in and out of the house, slamming the door and making the toddler in the cradle cry. Cissy held another, younger baby to her breast. And if Dee's eyes were telling her right, the woman was in the family way again. Gran wouldn't be happy about that. Last baby, Cissy had swollen up until she was almost unrecognizable by the time of her confinement. Gran had told her and Cissy's husband, Ray, the source of the ginger hair, not to have any more children, but what woman ever had a choice in that? Cissy also, Dee saw, sported a purple bruise on the side of her face. Something else in which women had little choice.

"Didn't duck fast enough," Cissy said, noticing Dee staring at her face.

But that was all she would say. Cissy never talked badly about her husband. Ray Price was an offshoot of the family that had first settled the area and given the village its name. Like all trees, family ones included, there were branches that twisted sideways from the rest. Ray was one of those. Despite the prohibition against alcohol, he always seemed to find a drink somewhere, and it turned him ugly. Cissy had such a sweet face; how anyone could even think to hit it, to leave purple bruises upon it, was beyond Dee's comprehension.

"How are you today, Defiance?" Cissy asked.

"Fine." Dee rocked the cradle, making soothing sounds so the little girl would settle. "Did you hear about the bones?" she asked.

"That's all anyone's talking about," Cissy said.

Despite the children and house to keep, Cissy still managed to know everything that was going on in Price's Corners.

"Do they have any idea who they belong to?"

"If they do, they aren't saying," Cissy replied. "I heard Chief O'Brien was looking for Dr. Hughes to go up the mountain to examine the bones before they were moved, but the doctor was at the mill. Someone got his hand caught in a machine. Not Ray, though. He sent word he was fine. Chief O'Brien wasn't too happy, though, to be standing around waiting on the doctor, but what else can he do?" She shifted the baby to her other breast. "I see the old Martin home has people living in it," she went on, changing the subject.

"That old place?" Dee was surprised. "It doesn't even have a proper roof!"

The old Martin house was her and Gran's closest neighbour, though it had long been empty and was said to be haunted by old man Martin, who didn't want to leave his home even in death. Dee and Billy had gone in one gloomy day on a dare from each other. Clooey had stood at the gate, wringing her hands in despair of ever seeing them again. But all Dee and Billy encountered were a couple of birds nesting in the rafters and a collapsed roof letting in the damp. She'd neither *seen*, nor *felt*, a ghost. Old man Martin wasn't there any longer, but whether he had been dragged kicking and screaming or went on to the other world of his own accord, Dee didn't know.

"A widow woman I heard," Cissy said. "Her husband died of influenza, leaving her and her children poor." Cissy looked around her kitchen with satisfaction. "I'm glad I have a decent roof over my head and food for my children."

Dee looked away from the cradle—the baby had finally closed her eyes—and again took in Cissy's bruised cheek. She guessed it was worth it to have a man provide for you. Cissy was right, many women were on their own for the first time in their lives thanks to the war and the influenza epidemic that followed, and they were having a hard time of it.

The war. At first the mountain had shielded Price's Corners from the war. The village people read about it in the newspapers, but it was an ocean away, in Europe. Eventually, though, even the mountain couldn't keep the young men home. First a trickle and then a stream of men left the farms and towns, heading to the city and a uniform, and ultimately for a foreign place across the Atlantic Ocean. Billy's father had gone, as had Constable Carter, Clooey's dad, Dr. Hughes, and most of the men from the woollen mill, leaving only a few, including Ray Price—more the pity for Cissy—to carry on farming or making blankets for the soldiers. The war changed so many lives. Husbands, sons, and fathers were buried a long way from home, women were made widows too early, and children were left fatherless.

And the lucky ones who did return from the fighting? Many came home coughing up rotted lungs, while others left limbs and sometimes their minds behind in France—like Clooey's dad. He came back barely able to breathe and now sat in a chair all day staring at nothing. Clooey confided in Dee that she believed that the man who returned home from the war was not her father, especially as the man couldn't recall her name at times. Clooey was convinced they had taken in a stranger. Dee had repeated this to Gran, who said that was nonsense, and she, Gran, should know the man was Clooey's father because she'd been at his birth. Still, Clooey refused to call him "father," referring to him instead as "Mister," a name Dee now used.

Constable Carter and Dr. Hughes seemed to come through the war fine, though Billy's father lost all ten of his toes to trench foot. Billy said his dad stuffed the insides of his shoes with paper to make up for the loss of the digits and got around all right.

And then influenza followed right on the heels of the returning soldiers, killing even more people, and this time right there in Price's Corners. For weeks, Dee hadn't gone to school or church. Gran had nursed people wherever she could but wouldn't let Dee go with her. "It's the young who are dying," she said. "Not the elderly." Dee doubted there was a family in the area untouched by the war or the sickness.

"What did you learn at school today, Defiance?" Cissy asked.

Dee shrugged. "Miss Hamilton told us about the Rocky Mountains. She said they were different from *our* mountain."

Cissy laughed. "You mean *your* mountain. We used to think that way, too, your mama and I. We used to play on *our* mountain all the time when we were youngsters. Now it's *your* mountain to play on. She was so much fun, your mama. Always getting me in trouble with her grand ideas. You're the spitting image of her, Defiance." She sighed and looked at the brood of children sitting around the table, waiting for their supper. "Seems so long ago."

Dee loved hearing about Mama, loved thinking that maybe she and Mama had walked the very same paths, put their foot down on the very same spot on the mountain.

Dee had to admit that at times she found it hard to forgive Mama for just up and going, and leaving her, Dee, behind. But at the same time, she understood how a person might want to see different things, wake up one morning and leave to wander the world. A world that was much more exciting than staying in Price's Corners and taking care of a baby beneath the village's unkind eyes. Gossip and Gran. That's what had driven Mama away.

She set plates on the table for the children's supper. "Miss Hamilton says the Rocky Mountains are so high that the tops are in the clouds and all year long the peaks have snow on them."

Cissy buttoned her dress front and placed the baby beside the other in the cradle. "That must be something to see," she murmured.

"I'd like to go to those mountains someday," Dee said. It surprised her how her voice came out all mad and determined.

CHAPTER THREE

"I told you to come straight home from school, Grand-daughter," Gran said. She was packing her birthing bag, setting in fresh sheets, towels, scissors, needle and thread, baby clothing, vinegar, and small packages of herbs.

"I stopped to see Cissy," Dee said.

Gran's hands stilled. "How is she?"

Dee knew exactly what Gran was asking. "She's fine, I guess. She's got a big bruise on her face, but she doesn't seem overly bothered," then added, "I think she's also expecting again."

Gran shook her head. "It will be the death of her." She folded white strips of sheeting for bandages. "Maggie Forgetti is ready."

Dee's interest stirred. Maggie's husband was Italian. The story went that he came through Price's Corners in 1906 with a travelling show, saw Maggie in the audience and fell instantly in love, and the show moved on without him. He was the only Italian in the area, olive-skinned, with black-haired arms and dark eyes. Some people thought he was shifty because he spoke differently from them. During the war, those same people had wanted him locked up, saying he was a spy. But the war had ended last year without him seeing the inside of a cell. He and Maggie and eight black-eyed, black-headed children lived happily on a farm a fair distance down Mountain View Road.

"Did Maggie send a message?" Dee asked.

"No," Gran said abruptly.

That meant that Gran had a *feeling* Maggie was ready to give birth. The same type of *feeling* she told Dee to ignore.

"Get your things together. We'll be there a couple of nights. Mr. Forgetti will be arriving shortly to pick us up." Gran must have had a *feeling* about that also.

"Teacher says I have to hand in an essay by week's end," Dee said. "I could stay here and work on it while you go. Miss Hamilton says I miss too much school."

"You can work on it while we're at the Forgettis and hand it in on Monday. That will have to suit Miss Hamilton. I need your help," Gran told her.

Dee sighed. She would miss the rest of the week of school. Sometimes Gran didn't know the trouble she got Dee into. With eight Forgetti children needing care and a ninth being born, Dee wouldn't have time to work on an essay.

"Some people moved in to the old Martin place," Dee said.

"A widow," Gran replied. "She's going to try her hand at dressmaking. She should have settled in Wallen."

Dee knew what Gran meant. Price's Corners women made their own clothes and those for their family. There wasn't extra money to pay a seamstress.

"Lots of women are in her position right now," Gran went on. "She looks scared as a rabbit and about as useful. She needs to pull herself together for her children's sake."

It figured that Gran would know all about their new neighbours. It seemed that everyone knew everything before Dee did.

"I told them to use our well until they get their own cleaned out. There's a girl, looks about your age. The girl . . ." Gran's voice trailed off and Dee turned to see her grandmother staring at the wall. Suddenly, Gran frowned and then briskly snapped shut her bag.

"There's no roof," Dee said.

"That's why she got it so cheap. I asked Billy's father to see to it," Gran replied. "Now, get your clothes together, girl."

When Mr. Forgetti arrived, his eyebrows rose in surprise to find them packed and ready to go. "I knew it was close to Maggie's time and kept us ready," was all Gran said in answer to his unasked question.

Mr. Forgetti said nothing but helped Gran up onto the wagon seat, placing her birthing bag carefully at her feet. In Price's Corners, most people ignored Gran's *gift*, grateful for her skill with birthing and her advice for their rheumatism, croup, or other ailments. On the other hand, if someone's crop blackened or a healthy cow just up and died, Dee saw the sideways glances her grandmother received. Still others laughed or talked about Gran's *gift* with scorn, though Dee could tell tales about how those very same skeptics made their way through the night to knock on their door with requests for a love potion to tame a wandering husband, syrup to calm a cough the doctor couldn't subdue, teas to relieve pain during their woman's days—or with desperate appeals for another sort of help. When those came, Gran would tell Dee to go to bed, though one time she watched through a crack in the door to see the woman's tears, hear her pleas and Gran speaking soothingly but shaking her head. Later when she understood, Dee was glad her grandmother would not provide that sort of help.

Dee crawled into the back of the wagon and made herself comfortable, stretching her legs out in front of her and shifting a large bag of flour to use as a backrest. Mr. Forgetti had obviously been in Wallen picking up supplies. It would be a two-hour wagon ride around the mountain, but Dee didn't mind. It wasn't often she got an opportunity to just sit and be with her own thoughts.

The wagon headed toward the base of the mountain, arriving at the split in the road just as Chief O'Brien, Constable Carter, and Billy's father walked over the footbridge, a white-sheeted stretcher between them. Dr. Hughes followed, black bag in hand, trailed by Reverend McAllister.

The bones, Dee realized.

Mr. Forgetti pulled back on the horses and the wagon stopped. "You need help?" he asked.

"No," answered Chief O'Brien. They carried the stretcher over to Billy's father's wagon. "Take those to Dr. Hughes's office in Wallen," he ordered.

Unable to look away, Dee stared at the small bulges in the sheet but couldn't make sense of either a human or animal body. She shivered suddenly and glanced away. That was when she saw the pillar of black, opaque and as tall as the trees, churning on the path behind the men. Unaware, they must have carried the bones right past it, unless . . . unless it had followed them down from the mountain.

"Gran," she whispered.

"Be still," her grandmother murmured.

Gran couldn't *see* the dead like Dee could, but she could sense them. Gran's particular gift was *knowing* what ailed a person just by looking at them, or *knowing* what might happen beforehand, like Maggie's baby coming.

But this, this thick, dark shadow, was like no spirit Dee had seen before, if spirit it even was. Her insides quivered. With some effort she kept herself from leaping off the wagon and running far away.

"Mrs. Vale, Dee." Dr. Hughes touched the brim of his hat, then twirled the ends of his moustache while he considered Gran. He knew she was off to a birthing, and he didn't like it.

He wouldn't say anything, though, for today there had been an accident at the mill, and now the bones—leaving no time for a baby.

"Will we see you in church on Sunday, Mrs. Vale?" Reverend McAllister asked. He was a short man with a round stomach, his bald head presently concealed beneath his flat black hat. His eyes glared at the world as he confronted its many sins.

"No," Gran said.

Reverend McAllister sighed. "And Defiance?" he said.

"She'll be there as always," Gran said.

Despite Dee's protests at having to sit alone in a pew for all to see—the girl who didn't have a father and whose mother had abandoned her—Gran insisted that Dee go to church. In the long run, Gran explained, it was better to endure a bit of gossip now than to not go and add fuel to simmering fires. Dee felt she could reconcile herself to that except for the fact that Gran herself wouldn't go because of an old falling-out with Reverend McAllister. What that was about, her grandmother kept to herself.

But these thoughts flitted swiftly through Dee's head because from the corner of her eye she continued to watch the unmoving pillar, terrified to look at it straight on.

"We'll be on our way, then." Mr. Forgetti snapped the reins on the horses' backs and turned to follow the road to the right. Dee let out a shaky breath. She badly wanted to talk to Gran about what she'd seen, but it would be a while before they had a minute alone.

"In town, the talk is all about the bones," Mr. Forgetti said—to Dee's ear, it sounded like "*een* town" and "*eez* all."

Dee settled back, willing herself to relax as she listened to him. Mr. Forgetti's accent reminded her that there were other languages and other people leading lives in places other than Price's Corners. She had seen the map at school, but it didn't seem real, with the world laid out flat and coloured blue, pink, and yellow. Dee had found Italy, a country shaped like a boot, and marvelled at the wide expanse of water, the Atlantic Ocean, that Mr. Forgetti had travelled across by ship to get to Canada.

"People saying them bones, they not that old," Mr. Forgetti continued.

"Someone who got lost on the mountain," Gran said firmly.

Mr. Forgetti stole a look at Dee's grandmother, saw the grim set of her mouth, and knew talk about the bones had ended.

Dee firmly pushed the bones and the black column to the back of her mind and turned her thoughts to her mother again.

The story, as Dee believed and Gran had never disputed, was that Mama, who loved to sing, had left to join a travelling music show.

On the shelf above the kitchen window sat a seashell with rough brown and white ridges on the outside and a pearl-white inside that was the smoothest surface Dee's fingers had ever touched. Mama had sent that to her, a note accompanying it saying, *I found this on the beach and thought of you. Put the shell to your ear and you'll hear the ocean.* Dee had done that right away and, sure enough, she heard the sound of waves breaking on sand. The second time she'd held the shell to her ear, she heard the call of seabirds.

Then one day she'd sniffed the shell and smelled salt. Another time, it stank of fish, ocean fish; more exotic than those she and Billy caught in Dickson Creek.

Lately, though, Dee looked at the shell infrequently because the sight of it brought such a puzzling sense of loss that it left her sad for days. Why didn't Mama ever come back to see her now that she was nearly grown? In her heart Dee knew why. It was because she, Dee, wasn't good enough, not important enough for Mama to leave her exciting life and come to see her. It came back to disappointment. She was a disappointment to her mother.

Sitting beside the shell on the shelf was a photograph of Gran, tall and thin, smooth-faced in her wedding clothes, next to an even taller man. His jacket sleeves were too short: probably a suit borrowed for the special day. Both looked very serious, but if she peered close, Dee thought that she could see happiness glowing in Gran's eyes. The tall man, Dee's grand-father, had died of pneumonia when Dee's mother was twelve years old. Cissy had told Dee that and also of the tears Dee's mother had cried for days for her father.

"And Gran?" Dee had asked. "Did she cry, too?"

"Not that I saw," Cissy had said. "I think your gran is the type to hold that in," she had added.

Dee had never seen Gran cry. Even when a sweet baby was born still, without breath, and Dee's own eyes welled up, Gran never cried. She just set her mouth firmer.

The wagon bounced over a hard rut, rattling Dee's teeth together. Mr. Forgetti turned and smiled an apology. Dee's stomach rumbled and she sighed, knowing that if there was to be a supper for her tonight, she'd be the one to cook it and she'd be the one to feed the children before she could get a bite herself.

An autumn chill set in with the growing darkness. Night came early on the east side of the mountain, though sun-pinked clouds still hung overhead. The road was narrower here, close-packed red and white oak, sugar maple, and beech trees crowding right to the ditch. There were secret places beneath the trees, Dee knew; places of shadow and cool damp, revealed when the wind stripped away the leaves to lay the branches bare. Was that why the bones had been found now? Because the mountain was giving up its secrets along with its foliage? *Secrets and secret places beneath the trees.* Something just on the edge of her mind. A tree. If only she could grasp it.

"You might want to hurry those horses up a bit," Gran said suddenly.

And Dee's train of thought was broken.

Without questioning why, Mr. Forgetti urged the horses into a quick walk. The wagon swayed from side to side. An owl screeched from the woods, stalking its prey; from the ditch, a rustle in the long grasses, a small creature disturbed and scampering away to the shelter of the trees. Other things moved within those trees, too, Dee knew. Things that roamed the mountain, slipping from shadow to shadow so quickly you weren't sure if they were real or a play of light. Most people thought ghosts came out only at night. Dee knew better. They were always present. She wasn't afraid of them. She had long ago discovered that most haunts were too caught up in their own anguished reasons for clinging to this world to bother with the earthly likes of her. When she first had become aware of them, Dee couldn't rightly say. Perhaps it was the time when she was four and Mrs. Miller from the livery in Price's Corners had come to see Gran about her husband's shortness of breath. Dee could see the shimmering outline of a man behind the woman, standing in the kitchen doorway.

"I'm sorry," Dee said.

"About what?" the woman asked.

"That he's dead," Dee replied, puzzled. Couldn't Mrs. Miller see his haunt standing right there?

"Never mind my granddaughter," Gran had said. "She's playing." And Gran had shooed Dee out of the room.

Sure enough, they soon received word that Mrs. Miller

had returned home to discover that her husband had died in her absence. Folks talked about Dee for a while after that.

Only once had a spirit scared Dee. When she was eight, she had rushed home from playing on the mountain with Billy and Clooey to tell Gran about a weeping woman she'd seen wandering in the woods, long skirt sweeping the pine-needle floor and a rope looped around her neck, the frayed end of which trailed down her bodice. She also told Gran that her own neck hurt, much like the woman's must with that rope around it. That pain and the woman's hopelessness had scared Dee.

"Should we help her, Gran?" she had asked.

Gran had taken Dee by the shoulders, given her a shake. "Don't talk such nonsense. There was no one there. You saw a tree stump. That's all. You didn't see anything." Gran's voice was harsh.

Cowed by Gran's stern words, Dee secretly watched Billy and Clooey whenever they all played to see if they noticed the odd shadows in the forest. She soon realized they didn't. *She* was the one who was different. It was her shame alone.

CHAPTER FOUR

D ee yawned. It had been a long night, and it wasn't over
yet. She opened the stove and put another stick of wood
on the fire, then placed the kettle on top to boil. They were on
their fourth pot of tea.

They'd arrived to find Maggie in bed, teeth chattering,
bulbous stomach convulsing, and the children running wild
despite the efforts of the eldest, a boy of twelve, to keep
them in line. Dee fed and put the children to bed, swept the
kitchen floor, and kept the stove hot, while Gran tended to
Maggie.

From outside came the *crack* of an axe splitting wood as
Mr. Forgetti worked through his worry. Worried enough, Dee
judged, to keep the family warm for the larger part of the winter. She poured a cup of tea and took it out to him. He looked
up expectantly as she approached, but she shook her head. He
leaned on his axe and took the tea.

"Soon, right?"

"It shouldn't be long now," Dee assured him, though she

really didn't know. It was just something you said to the husband to make him feel better. She looked up at the sky, at the
silver stars, and took a deep breath of cold air, expelling it in a
puff of white.

"There are women in Italy like Mrs. Vale," Mr. Forgetti
said.

"What do you mean?" Dee asked.

"Old women," he answered. "They know things. They dress
all in black. Black head"—he made the motion of tying on
a kerchief—"to their black feet. They deliver our babies, too.
And do other things. You don't want to get on the wrong side
of them."

Dee smiled and went back into the house. Gran came out
of the bedroom. "It shouldn't be long now," she said.

Dee heard a low moan from behind the partially closed
door. Maggie was labouring hard to get that baby born.

"I am never getting married," Dee announced.

Gran raised her eyebrows.

"At least not until the Lord sees fit to have men share in
the child-bearing," Dee continued.

For a wonder, Gran smiled, and for a fleeting instant Dee
saw the beautiful woman in the wedding photograph.

"You'll feel differently when you're older," Gran said.

"I don't think so," Dee said. "I'm already fourteen. Maggie
had her first baby at seventeen. Mama had me at fifteen."

Gran's mouth tightened at the mention of Dee's mother.

"I want to go to high school and learn," Dee said. "I don't mind being a spinster."

"Don't be so silly," Gran said. "All girls want to be married. Now, take a cup of tea in to Maggie. Just let her sip it, mind. I'm going to see to getting some towels."

Dee opened the door and tiptoed into the bedroom. Maggie smiled briefly, face pale from exhaustion. As Dee wiped the woman's face with a wet cloth, another contraction took hold of her.

"You have a gentle touch," Maggie said when the contraction was over. "It feels warm and . . ." She struggled to find the right word. "Peaceful." She grabbed Dee's hand and held it to her cheek. "Peaceful," she whispered.

Dee heard a noise behind her and turned to see Gran standing at the door watching, a look of satisfaction on her face. She knew exactly what Gran was thinking. Well, Gran could think again because Dee was not going to be a midwife, stuck forever in Price's Corners.

She moved to leave the bedroom.

"Stay," Gran ordered. "Maggie finds it a comfort having you here."

Maggie managed a quick smile and a nod before another contraction overtook her. She gripped Dee's hand. Gran laid a hand on Maggie's abdomen. "You can push now, Maggie," she said. "Raise her shoulders up," she ordered Dee.

Gran washed her hands carefully, scrubbing around and

under the fingernails. "The cleaner everything is, the better. It keeps the mother well afterward," she had often told Dee.

From outside came the steady chop of Mr. Forgetti's axe, drowned momentarily by a cry from Maggie. Then things moved so quickly that even later, when Dee had a moment to ponder on it, she couldn't recall the actual birth. One moment she was holding Maggie's hand, the next wrapping a new baby boy in a clean towel as Gran tidied up the birthing room in the soft, grey light of dawn. Gran left the room, and soon the chop of axe cleaving wood stopped.

There was no time for sleep for Dee, as Maggie's children were waking. Each one crept in to see their new brother, their jaws dropping at how small he was and thinking Dee was lying when she told them that they, too, had been so tiny when they were born.

Finally, Gran chased everyone from the room, and she and Dee left Maggie and Mr. Forgetti alone to marvel at their new son.

Despite their hard night, Gran stoked the stove and put kettles of water on to warm while Dee dragged out the laundry tub. Thankfully, Mr. Forgetti had made sure his wife had a decent tub, one with a handle that turned and scrubbed the clothes, so she didn't need to launder them by hand. It would make Dee's job of washing for the large family a little easier.

Gran chopped vegetables for a stew and made biscuits.

They would stay for a couple of days to give the new mother a chance to rest.

Something else was simmering along with the stew, Dee soon realized: her temper. She was simmering up a huge anger. Finally it came to a boil.

"I'm not going to be a midwife," she burst out.

Gran opened the oven door and peeked at the biscuits.

"Did you hear me? I'm not going to be a midwife. And it doesn't matter how much you act like I am, I'm still not. Women are going to go to doctors and maternity homes and hospitals to have their babies," Dee said. "They won't need midwives."

"And how are they going to get there?" Gran asked.

"By truck and car," Dee replied. "Soon everyone will have trucks and cars. Not just the rich people. That's what Dr. Hughes says."

"And what do men doctors know about birthing babies?" Gran said disgustedly. "Women birth babies, not men. Having babies is natural. Doctors come around and suddenly women think they are sick and having babies is an illness."

"Maybe there will be women doctors soon," Dee said, the idea just occurring to her. She turned the notion around in her head and discovered she quite liked it. Women doctors.

Gran turned from the stove and looked at Dee. "You have hands that know how to give comfort. That's a gift."

"Not one I asked for," Dee said. She wasn't quite sure why

she was arguing so heatedly with Gran. It might not even be about being a midwife. It was just—she didn't like the feeling that Gran was planning her life for her without any say from Dee! She knew she had a comforting way with ill people. In fact, her grandmother would be surprised to find the newspaper clipping Dee kept beneath her pillow. She had come upon it last year and since then had looked at it so often that the newsprint was now limp and worn. *Pupil nurses needed!* the advertisement read, an advertisement all the way from a hospital in Chicago.

Dee piled wet clothes in a bushel basket and settled it on her hip, pulled open the door, and went outside to hang overalls and shirts on Maggie's clothesline. It took her a long time, since the younger children ran around her legs snatching the clothes as she tried to peg them; it was a wonderful game—to them at least. As Dee rescued one of Mr. Forgetti's shirts before it landed in the pigpen, she thought again about the advertisement.

It said that the pupil nurses would train for two years. She believed Dr. Hughes when he said that soon more and more people would be going to hospitals and that that was where the care would be given, to rich and poor alike. And she wanted to be part of that. They would take her as a student. She knew more about taking care of people than most girls her age, and she wasn't at all squeamish. Perhaps she would talk to Dr. Hughes about being a pupil nurse. It was scary and exciting all at the same time to think of being away from Price's Corners. And, Dee thought, no one would know her in Chicago; no one would know she didn't have a father and that her mother had left her. No one would know that she was different, that she could *see* and *feel* what others could not.

CHAPTER FIVE

Dee was bone-weary when Mr. Forgetti dropped them at their house on Saturday, along with a squealing piglet, a load of chopped wood, two jars of raspberry preserves, and profuse thanks for the healthy baby boy. Late-afternoon sun stretched the tree trunks into long, thin shadows as Dee climbed down from the wagon. All she wanted to do was sleep for the rest of the day and into the night. Unexpectedly, Gran told her to go to bed and she'd see to settling the new pig in the pen with Trojan and completing the remainder of the chores. Billy had been by to feed the chickens, taking any eggs he could find to his mother as payment for doing so, leaving one less chore to be done.

Carrying the preserves, Dee went through the gate and rounded the house to the back porch. She stopped at the sight of a girl pulling water from their well. The new neighbour. Blonde hair hung in unwashed strings to the middle of her back. Her skirt was too short for her long legs and her blouse too tight across her chest, as if the girl had had a sudden growth spurt but no new clothes to keep up with it. Despite these shortcomings, Dee could see that the girl was quite pretty, beautiful really. She stared at Dee with eyes of washed, pale blue, not a friendly stare, but not an unfriendly one either, just indifferent. After a moment, Dee nodded, then climbed the steps and went inside, too tired to puzzle over a strange girl's empty stare.

She fell into bed fully dressed and immediately into sleep, a sleep haunted with dreams of white bones and crying babies.

A knock on the front door, a few hours later, woke her. Dee lay drowsily and listened to the murmur of voices, wondering idly who needed her grandmother's skills now. Then she heard Gran's voice rise in anger. That pulled Dee from the warmth of her bed. She opened the bedroom door a crack. Her grandmother stood in the front doorway, blocking Dee's view. Night had fallen while she had slept, leaving her with no sense of the time.

"She's sleeping, and I'm not waking her so you can bother her with useless questions," she heard Gran say.

A hinge creaked as Dee opened the door wider, curious to see who her grandmother was speaking to so harshly.

"Well, she's awake now," a man's voice said.

Dee blinked and rubbed her eyes as she walked toward the door. Gran didn't move her thin frame, so Dee stood on the tips of her toes and saw Chief O'Brien and Dr. Hughes on the top step and, pacing nervously up and down the front path, Constable Carter. The two police officers were in their navy uniforms, though the chief's stretched tight across his heavy paunch.

"Defiance . . ." Chief O'Brien used her full name, so Dee knew it was serious. "I have something here that I was wondering if you could identify for us." He held out his fist and uncurled his fingers.

Dee pushed under her grandmother's arm to get a closer look. Resting on his palm was a red-stoned ring.

"This was on the finger bone of the skeleton we found up on the mountain."

Dr. Hughes studied Dee's face closely while the constable crowded the two men to peer at the ring himself.

Dee reached for it, but Gran grabbed her arm and yanked it back. "Don't touch that ring," she barked.

Chief O'Brien glared at Gran's interference. Dee folded her hands together, fighting the temptation to reach out a second time. She knew the ring all right, the blood-red stone, though she hadn't seen or even thought about it for over four years. Nor about the girl who had worn it, Mary Ann Simpson, whose parents owned the Mercantile.

"Do you know anything about this?" Dr. Hughes asked gently. He plucked it from the chief's hand and held it up to Dee. A sharp pain went through Dee's head. She gasped.

"Do you want to see it up close?" Dr. Hughes held it between his thumb and finger.

Gran gripped Dee's shoulder, not letting her move forward. "She can see it just fine."

Dee knew why Gran was so insistent that she not touch the gold band or stone. Even this far away she could feel the tug, the violence swirling around it. The men were bringing something terrible to their home. The sooner they left, the better. She'd tell them whose hand she'd last seen it on and they'd go, and leave her and Gran alone. That would be the end of it.

"It's Mary Ann Simpson's."

Chief O'Brien took the ring back from Dr. Hughes and dropped it into a small brown envelope. "That's what we figured," he said. "But people say you were her best friend and we thought you'd know for sure if it was hers. Mrs. Vale, we need to come in and speak to Dee."

Dee's grandmother reluctantly stepped aside, and the men filed in. They settled themselves around the kitchen table. Gran grudgingly poured the ever-present tea for everyone and pushed a plate of cornbread and a dish of Maggie's preserves toward them. She might not like having them there, but she'd not have them say the Vales kept a poor house. Constable Carter's eyes darted about the room.

"Are you looking for anything in particular?" Gran asked.

The constable blushed. Everyone knew what he was looking for: witches' brews and potions. Dee almost wished they had bat heads and lizard tails drying over the hearth so he wouldn't be disappointed. And it really was too bad that Gran couldn't turn him into a toad, as he was already halfway there, with his bulgy eyes and red tongue flicking constantly over thick, meaty lips.

Dr. Hughes crossed his legs, one hand straying to his waxed and painstakingly curled moustache. Dee could imagine him stroking it wisely as he told his patients all about their dire ills. Chief O'Brien shifted his bulk, trying to find comfort on the hard wooden chair. He, too, had a moustache, bushy and unkempt.

"You got new neighbours," Chief O'Brien said, the drink and food requiring social niceties before he got down to business.

"Yes," Gran said shortly, and then reluctantly added, "A woman and her children. Alone. Her man died in the epidemic."

Chief O'Brien nodded. "Lots of families in the same situation right now. I saw an older girl when we passed. Looks about your age, Dee. A new friend for you." This gave him the opening he needed.

"Tell us everything you know about Mary Ann Simpson," Chief O'Brien began. "Right up until the last time you saw her. Constable Carter here will take notes of what you say, if you don't mind—now that he's finished examining the kitchen," he added dryly.

Constable Carter quickly pulled a small notebook from the breast pocket of his dark blue uniform, licked the end of a

lead pencil and sat, ready. Dee studied him, giving herself time
to think about what to say. Gran said Constable Carter had
an exaggerated opinion of himself; that he swaggered about
the village but at heart was a true coward, quick to back down
when cornered. He was behaving himself now with Chief
O'Brien sitting across from him.

Dr. Hughes took a sip of his tea. At least he wasn't afraid
to drink it like Dee knew Constable Carter was. The police
officer was eyeing his cup with suspicion, keeping his distance.
He was also hungrily eyeing the cornbread. Dr. Hughes was
more modern. He didn't believe in superstitions or that Gran
was a witch. He'd studied medicine in the city and had worked
there for a couple of years before he married and set up a
practice in Wallen. People at the time wondered why a smart,
young doctor would want to bury himself and his pretty wife
in the country, but he'd been in Wallen nearly sixteen years
now, so he must find it agreeable.

"Dee?" the chief said.

"I don't know. We were friends." Dee shrugged.

"She was a little old to be your friend, wasn't she?" Dr.
Hughes asked.

Dee shrugged again. There had been a four-year difference
between her and Mary Ann, but they had got along fine. "We
weren't best friends. Clooey's always been my best friend."

"Children around here all play together no matter their
age," Gran put in.

Chief O'Brien nodded. He knew that to be true.

"Mary Ann liked to go up the mountain, but she was always getting turned around and lost, so she'd ask me to go with her. She was nice."

"When did you first see the ring on her finger?" Chief O'Brien asked.

Dee didn't know why she was having so much trouble dredging up this information. It was as if there was a wall holding it back. She pushed hard against the barrier and broke through to find bits and pieces of Mary Ann Simpson. Light brown hair, wide hazel eyes, a shapely figure early, and, at fourteen, well on her way to becoming a plump woman like her mother. As a village girl, Mary Ann didn't have a lot of outdoor chores to take up her time and always had nice clothes to wear and toys to play with.

Mary Ann wasn't especially bright, Dee realized, surprised that she'd known that even back when they'd played together. The older girl mooned around a lot, sighing tragically, her head filled with nonsense from reading her mother's romantic novels. *And the tree*; the tree that had tried to force its way into Dee's memory on the way to the Forgettis, a tall spruce with plentiful lower branches to conceal the girls, and beneath, soft needles to sit upon. A special place just for them. Dee suddenly remembered how under the tree Mary Ann would make Dee play servant to her princess. Dee had been happy to take the lesser role because the princess had two baby dolls with china heads and hands, and beautiful clothes, and it was the servant's job to care for the babies. She did this carefully, tucking them into leafy bowers and checking that four-legged and, occasionally, two-legged thieves didn't make off with them. She told the chief about that. And about how all at once Mary Ann ignored the dolls, even going so far as to tell Dee she could keep one. Dee had been delighted to have such a fine gift, but Gran—Dee flicked a hurt glance toward her grandmother—had made her give it back, saying it was too expensive a gift for Dee.

Greed winning over fear, Constable Carter suddenly leaned forward, took a slice of cornbread, spread it thickly with preserves, and shoved it in his mouth, crumbs raining onto his tunic. Dr. Hughes regarded the constable with open disgust.

Chief O'Brien shook the ring from the envelope and laid it in the middle of the table.

"And this?" he asked.

"The last time I saw Mary Ann was the end of August four years ago. We went up the mountain. We went to the tree," Dee said. She could remember it clearly now.

Clouds shrouded the peak and crept down the slopes, obliterating the trail in front of them as they climbed upward. It had rained earlier in the morning, and warm, humid air hugged the ground; it was almost too thick to breathe.

"I have something to show you," Mary Ann said. "But we have to be away from everyone. No one can know. It's a secret."

Dee was delighted, excited by the dripping trees, white mist, and mostly, the impending secret. She led the way up, stopping at times to make sure that Mary Ann was following her. The other girl could never find their special place despite being there umpteen times. At last they pushed inside a thick-branched spruce and settled on the dry, brown needles.

Dee hugged her knees and waited in the semi-darkness of their shelter, anticipating.

"You can't tell anyone," Mary Ann said.

"Cross my heart," Dee said. She wished Mary Ann would get on with it, but the girl drew out the moment, enjoying the suspense.

"I'm engaged," she said finally.

Dee frowned.

"Engaged to be married, silly." Mary Ann held out her left hand. On her third finger was a ring. "You can't tell anyone yet. He said not to."

"Who?" Dee asked.

"I can't tell you. That's a secret, too. But he's grown up. Not like those stupid boys at school. He's a man. I'll have my own house and my own family. I'm going to be a wife."

Dee was disappointed. It wasn't much of a secret. Wives were commonplace.

"He says he loves me." Mary Ann pulled the ring off her finger and threaded it through a white string that she then tied around her neck and tucked inside her blouse collar. "I can't show this yet. Now, remember. It's a secret."

Dee told Chief O'Brien and Dr. Hughes about that last conversation while Constable Carter scribbled furiously.

"So she didn't say who the man was?" Chief O'Brien asked.

"No," Dee said. "Just that he was a man, not a boy from school."

Dee stared at the ring, seeing its cheapness. Had Mary Ann seen that? Dee didn't think so. She'd handled it carefully like it was gold. But that ring, you could get one like it from any travelling peddler for a few pennies. "All Mary Ann said was that her prince had come," Dee said. "When I didn't see her anymore, I thought she had run away to get married. That's what people said in town. They said it broke her mother's heart, and Mrs. Simpson stopped working in the Mercantile. I sort of forgot about her."

All this time she'd thought Mary Ann was married, a wife with a family just liked she'd wanted, but instead the girl had been up on the mountain, flesh falling from bone.

"The tree you're talking about," Chief O'Brien said. "Was it on the far side of a clearing, about a half an hour climb?"

Dee nodded.

She wondered why the chief wanted to know, but he didn't offer any explanation for his question.

"It's interesting," Dr. Hughes said. "Neither of you have asked how Mary Ann died."

"I thought she just got lost up the mountain," Dee said.

"She was always getting turned around. Sometimes she'd be going up but thinking she was going down."

Gran took a moment, and when she spoke, Dee knew her grandmother was choosing her words carefully. "It stands to reason that dying that young and being healthy, the girl's death is bound to be unnatural, isn't it?"

"How did she die?" Dee asked.

"A blow to the head. Caved in half her skull," Constable Carter answered with relish.

Chief O'Brien shot him a furious look. Obviously that information wasn't for the public.

The men pushed back their chairs and slapped their hats on their heads. "Thank you for the tea, Mrs. Vale. It was good," Dr. Hughes said. "What did Maggie Forgetti have?"

"A boy," Gran said.

"You really should encourage the women around here to come to the maternity home," he said. "It's safer for them."

"They'll do what they want no matter what I say," Gran told him.

"Women should have their babies with doctors present these days. Having old grannies deliver their children is old-fashioned and dangerous," Dr. Hughes went on, half-heartedly. He knew Gran was a good midwife and that she helped take the burden off him. It was a big area for one doctor to serve.

"Your own girl disappeared, didn't she, Mrs. Vale? Dee's mother?" Chief O'Brien asked.

Gran stiffened. "She didn't disappear. She's working with a travelling show."

"She's a singer," Dee added. She glanced at the shell on the shelf, then averted her eyes when she realized the doctor had followed her glance. She wasn't sharing that shell with anyone. It was for her alone.

Dee watched the three men walk out to the road. They stopped for a moment, looked up at the mountain and exchanged a few words, and then went to their automobiles.

Gran stood behind her. "Those bones are going to cause nothing but trouble," she said.

CHAPTER SIX

O n Monday morning, Dee got up before light to finish
her Shakespeare essay. She had worked on it Sunday
after church, and there was just a bit left to write. She almost
had it done when Gran called her to feed Trojan, the new
piglet, and the chickens. She packed up her books and came
out of her small bedroom. She would put the last touches on
it at school during penmanship class. A little while later she
was glad to head for school, since Gran was prickly as rose
thorns this morning. Nothing about Dee suited her grandmother today, from the way she fed the chickens to the way
she spooned porridge into the breakfast bowls. Gran was
always like this on the day of her monthly visit to Wallen to
pick up provisions; grumpy before she left, and grumpy when
she returned.

Dee didn't know why the trip into town bothered Gran so
much. Dee always liked a chance to go to Wallen. But Gran
never invited Dee to go with her. Dee would just have to tiptoe
about until Gran returned to acting more like her usual self.

It was at times like these, with Gran clicking her tongue at Dee and stomping around the house, that Dee retreated into her daydream that Mama came home and they were the best of friends. She and Mama would go to the creek, dip their bare feet in its cool waters, and Dee would tell her about school, and Billy wanting to carry her books, and Clooey thinking her dad a stranger, and Gran wanting to keep her in Price's Corners, and how she, Dee, wanted to be a pupil nurse. And Mama in return would tell her how the mountains reached right up to heaven, and how endless the ocean was, and how the streets of New York City teemed with people. And then she'd tell Dee that she'd come back just for her, for Dee, so the two of them could travel the world together. But that was just a daydream, Dee knew. Stuff made up of fluff, as Gran would say.

As she passed the old Martin house, the new girl came out on the front porch and stared at Dee with her lifeless eyes.

"Are you going to school?" Dee asked. She thought it polite to stop.

The girl shrugged.

"My name is Dee. You can walk with me if you like."

"I'll have to bring my brothers and sisters," the girl said.

"Miss Hamilton, that's our teacher, she won't mind having extra students," Dee assured her.

The girl nodded and went back into the house. As she waited, Dee saw a man sitting in the shadows of the porch.

Obviously not their father, as he was dead, and besides, Dee's impression was of a youth. She waved, but he didn't appear to notice, so Dee dropped her hand. A few minutes later the girl reappeared, pushing a ragged group of children in front of her.

"I'm Vivien," the girl said. She rattled off the names of her two brothers, Ian and Mac, and her younger sister, Esther. The two boys said a sullen hello, but Esther smiled cheerfully. "You're pretty," she told Dee.

Dee felt her face become warm. It wasn't often she heard praise, especially for her looks.

A few steps away they met Billy. He had started to walk up the road toward them, wondering where Dee had got to.

"This is Vivien," Dee said.

"I'm Billy. Dee's my girlfriend."

"I am not," Dee denied hotly.

"Yes, you are. Ma says I may as well marry you as anybody because we've known each other all our lives and we get along fine."

"And that's a reason to marry?" Dee asked.

"As good as any," Billy said. "She says I should marry you even if you are a bit strange." He leaned in and kissed her on the lips before she realized what he was doing.

She pushed him away. "What did you do that for?"

"I get to kiss you if I'm going to marry you," Billy explained.

"We're not getting married. And you're not to kiss me," Dee protested. "And I'm not strange."

What was getting into everyone? Lately, love and marriage was all the older girls at school could talk about, sighing and making eyes at the boys at recess. And now Billy? She found it unsettling. She'd known Billy all her life and not once had he ever tried to kiss her.

"Vivien can be your girlfriend," she offered.

Vivien shrugged. "I don't mind."

Billy stared at the girl for a moment, sizing her up. Dee had to admit that, even through a layer of dirt, Vivien's beauty shone through. Obviously Billy thought so too, for he fell in step with Vivien and took the girl's hand. Dee felt a stab of annoyance. Some boyfriend: almost engaged to her and he takes up with the first girl who smiles sideways at him. And what kind of girl was Vivien to take up with the first boy who asked her? And one she'd just met? Not that it mattered at all to Dee. She had better things to do than to get married.

She marched on ahead, reaching Podge's house before the others.

"Hi, Dee," Podge said happily. "I made you something," he added shyly. He handed her a wooden chipmunk.

Dee turned the small figure every which way, amazed as always that Podge could capture the very soul of whatever creature he carved. The chipmunk looked ready to jump right out of her hand.

"Who's the retard?" one of Vivien's brothers asked, joining them.

"He's not a retard. He's Podge," Dee said. "I bet he's smarter than you."

"No retard is smarter than me," the boy claimed.

"Can you find your way up the mountain and back in the dark?" Dee asked. "Podge can. He knows where every single tree is and every single path through them. He could find his way on Pike's Mountain blindfolded."

"And he plays good football," Billy added loyally. "You always want to be on Podge's team at recess."

"Why do you call him Podge?" Vivien asked.

"Because he likes porridge so much," Billy said.

"Porridge for breakfast, porridge for lunch, porridge for supper," Podge sang.

"I like Podge," Esther said. She took his hand. "He can be my boyfriend."

Podge looked down at the girl and grinned.

"Billy tried to kiss Dee. She didn't like it, so he's Vivien's boyfriend now," Esther told him. "You should kiss me like a real boyfriend."

Podge clumsily bent and kissed Esther's cheek with a loud smack.

Dee had never seen Podge kiss anyone before. She didn't know what to think of this new family stirring up all her friends.

Billy held Vivien's hand all the way to school. It made Dee smart to see it. He needed taking down a peg or two.

"Chief O'Brien and Dr. Hughes were at our house last night. Asking questions about the bones," Dee said casually. This was something Billy couldn't possibly know.

"What kind of questions?" Billy said.

"They found a ring on a finger. A bone finger on the bone hand," Dee added. "They know who the bones belong to."

"Who?" Billy asked eagerly.

"Doesn't your dad know?" Dee said smugly. Then she relented. "They belong to Mary Ann Simpson." Dee turned to Vivien. "Mary Ann's parents own the Mercantile. She disappeared four years ago. I thought she'd run away to get married." The words tumbled out. "I used to play with her even though she was older than me. She was engaged. That's what the ring was for, an engagement ring. Except she didn't get married, she disappeared instead."

Billy's mouth fell open. Even Vivien showed interest for the first time since Dee had met her. Dee felt much happier.

At school, Clooey was waiting for Dee by the swings. Liking that for once she was in the know before anyone else, Dee introduced Vivien and her brothers and sister to Clooey.

"Podge is my boyfriend," Esther told Clooey. "And Billy is Vivien's boyfriend."

"Billy?" Clooey glanced at Dee.

"I'll tell you all about it at recess," Dee promised. "Along with lots of other news, but right now I have to take the children in to meet Miss Hamilton."

She looked forward to telling Clooey all about Vivien's family, Billy, Maggie Forgetti's baby, and the ring Chief O'Brien had brought. Except, she realized shamefully, that wasn't anything to be excited about. She looked over at the Mercantile. Mr. and Mrs. Simpson had probably just learned that their daughter was dead. Now Dee wished she hadn't told Billy and Vivien. She decided she wouldn't say anything more about the ring.

Inside the schoolhouse, Miss Hamilton asked Vivien where she and her family came from.

"Toronto," Vivien said. "We had a big school there," she added, looking around the classroom.

"Our dad died of influenza," added one brother, whom Dee now recognized as Ian. The one who'd called Podge a retard.

"Such a dreadful time." Miss Hamilton sighed deeply. "First the war, then the influenza."

Seeing the wistful look on Miss Hamilton's face, Dee wondered if the teacher had had a sweetheart, one who had gone off to war and never returned. She'd never thought of the teacher as anything but a teacher, certainly not a woman with a beau. This past year since the war ended and the sickness took so many, it was as if the entire world was mourning.

"We haven't gone much to school lately," Vivien said. "With Dad's passing, we've been moving around a lot. I don't know how long we will stay here. We don't stay long in most places."

"It must be hard for your poor mother," Miss Hamilton said. "No man to help out."

Dee thought of the young man sitting on Vivien's porch. Couldn't he help? But perhaps he had been injured like so many others in the war. Like Clooey's father, who moved only from chair to bed to chair, and even that took up what little breath his damaged lungs could produce.

Miss Hamilton suggested that Vivien sit with Dee to catch up on schoolwork. Clooey moved to an empty desk and Dee graciously shared her books with Vivien. The girl showed little interest in books and slates and chalk, content to sit and stare out the window and, occasionally, turn around to smile at Billy. Dee soon decided Vivien was just a silly girl and Billy was welcome to her.

And that is exactly what she told Clooey while they ate their lunch on the school steps. It was warm there, sheltered from the wind, with the sun beating directly down on them.

"I always thought you liked Billy," Clooey said.

"I like him, but I don't want to marry him," Dee said. Still, it had hurt that he had so quickly turned to Vivien. Pride, Gran would say. It was funny how there were two kinds of pride: one that kept your house clean and your clothes washed, and a stubborn pride that left you hurting.

On the way home from school, Dee walked fast, anxious to leave Vivien and Billy behind, but they kept pace with her, Billy pulling Vivien along by the hand. The children followed, Esther and Podge bringing up the rear, stopping to pick bouquets of late Queen Anne's lace and purple asters from the roadside.

Dee was tempted to turn in to Cissy's, but she figured Vivien and the others would just follow her right into Cissy's kitchen. Cissy had enough on her plate without unwanted company.

Esther ran up and held out the flowers to Vivien. "For your and Billy's wedding," she said.

Billy grinned widely. Honestly, Dee thought. Boys could be so dumb.

Esther walked alongside Dee. "Did your dad die, too?" she asked.

If there was one thing Dee hated, it was questions about her father. "No," she said shortly.

"Why do you live with your grandmother? Where's your mama?"

"She sings in a travelling show," Dee said. "She's the star," she added for good measure and had the pleasure of seeing Esther's eyes widen.

She steeled herself for further questions, but none came. Esther ran back to Podge and that was the end of it. Dee was relieved. She hated the shocked looks on people's faces when she told them that she didn't know anything about her father. She didn't think even Gran knew. She'd caught her grandmother studying Dee's face when she thought Dee wasn't looking, trying to figure out whose nose or eyes or mouth

Dee had, who around Price's Corners Dee looked like. Gran told Dee it didn't matter who her father was, Dee was Dee and knowing wouldn't change that. But Dee didn't agree. She didn't feel whole, but she couldn't put that feeling into words that her grandmother would understand.

Billy went to do his chores, and Vivien and the children ran into the old Martin place, so Dee found herself alone at her gate. She hastily dumped her school books and lunch pail in a heap on the ground and walked toward the mountain. Hopefully, Gran wasn't home from Wallen yet so Dee wouldn't be found out, but if Gran did find out, well, so be it. The mountain had been calling to her all day.

Her boots clattered on the wooden footbridge as she ran over it. With the weather so unusually dry, the stream was down to a trickle and any fish left would be buried in the mud. She began to climb the trail and was soon among tall tree trunks. Her feet *swished* through red and gold oak and maple leaves, stirring up a sharp scent of ripeness and decay. A cicada sang, fooled by the unseasonable heat into thinking it was still summer.

Dee came across a twisted apple tree, wizened fruit clinging to its branches. Hungry, she picked the two that she judged to be the least wormy. She could live out here without ever having to go into town, she told herself happily. The mountain could provide all she needed: shelter, food, and water for drinking.

Her feet carried her upward as she bit and chewed the tart apples. Eventually she stripped off her sweater, the exertion of climbing and the bright sun making her hot. She folded it over her arm as she scrambled up a rise and into a small clearing ringed by trees, the clearing Chief O'Brien had asked her about. She hadn't been here for a long time, nearly a year. Yellow dust from golden rod stuck to her navy serge skirt and brown burrs fastened themselves to her stockings as she pushed through the tall grasses. She stopped once to feel the velvet softness of a red sumac head. A swarm of birds suddenly rose in a silent black cloud, startling her. They circled once and then swooped away to the south. Dee watched the stragglers beat their wings hard to catch up, then continued on her way across the clearing.

On the far side, she stopped at the foot of a giant spruce tree. This had been her and Mary Ann's special place. She realized she hadn't been here since Mary Ann had disappeared. She parted the low-hanging green boughs, but made no move to go through them.

A shiver began at her toes, travelled up her legs to her chest, and continued up to her head. This was it. This was the place where Mary Ann's bones had been found. She could *feel* it.

Ignoring her trembling legs, she pushed her way through. She didn't want to be afraid. Not of the mountain. Beneath the boughs the ground was trampled, the dried needles pushed aside. Taking a deep breath, she walked over to a narrow, man-made trench. This was where Mary Ann's body had lain. Suddenly cold, Dee pulled her sweater on, but still her teeth chattered. It was utterly still beneath the tree. *As silent as the grave.*

After a long moment, Dee stepped forward and examined the ground near the tree's trunk. Something was missing. If Mary Ann had been killed here . . . . Dee tried to puzzle out what was bothering her.

"Is this where that girl's bones were found?"

Dee's heart nearly bounded from her chest. Vivien stood watching her, face expressionless. Did the girl feel nothing?

"You followed me up here," Dee shouted, anger and fear in her voice.

Vivien shrugged. "Just thought I'd see where you were going."

"I don't like people sneaking around behind me," Dee went on.

"So is this where that girl died?" Vivien kicked at the dead leaves and needles under the tree.

"Don't do that," Dee said sharply. It was disrespectful and dangerous to disturb the resting place of the dead. Gran had taught her that. "Walk softly," she'd told the young Dee when they'd gone to visit Grandpa's grave. "Show the proper respect and the dead will rest content."

"I'm not hurting anything," Vivien said. But she stopped kicking.

"We'd better go before it gets dark," Dee said, anxious to be away, away from this place that reeked of death.

"What's this?" Vivien asked. She bent and picked up a small object from under a leaf, holding it out for Dee to see.

Dee's heart lurched when she saw what Vivien held in the palm of her hand. "Nothing important," she said. She snatched it from the girl and thrust it deep in her pocket. Turning on her heel, she pushed her way through the boughs. She'd thought it was the tree that had blocked the sun's light but now saw dark clouds racing over the mountaintop.

"Weather's turning," she murmured. Summer was finally giving way to autumn.

She headed down the mountain, feet flying over the ground. She didn't bother to check whether Vivien followed, such was her urgency. Her neck pricked. Something watched. Her head swung left and right, nervous and searching, but she saw neither animal nor human. She put on a burst of speed as she reached the bottom and neared the footbridge. She didn't need special *feelings* to tell her she was in danger. The air stank of malevolence. She gagged on its stench. She would never, she vowed, go back to her and Mary Ann's secret place again.

CHAPTER SEVEN

Late that night, the storm roared down the mountain and slammed into the wooden house. Rain drummed steadily against Dee's bedroom window, pushed by fierce gusts of wind. It didn't cause her any concern. The house had stood up to worse. Her grandfather had built it for Gran when they first got married—built it solid. Inside were two bedrooms off the kitchen: a large one for Gran and a smaller one for Dee that had once been her mother's. Dee liked sleeping in the same bed her mother once had, liked to feel the hollow in the mattress under her back and imagining Mama lying in the same spot, dreaming.

The kitchen ran the length of the house and held a square table surrounded by four wooden chairs, all made by her grandfather. A second long, narrow work table with a lower and upper shelf was fitted beneath the window and was used to wash dishes, knead bread, and chop vegetables. A pie cupboard with upper glass doors stood in one corner, displaying Gran's wedding plates.

A wood stove used for heat and cooking, stood against the west wall, two cushioned rocking chairs pulled up to it, the only comfort in the house. Some houses, like Clooey's, had a "good room," used only when the minister came to visit or to hold a coffin; "a waste" Gran called it. She had no use for such a room and, instead, had asked her husband for a summer kitchen to be built onto the back of the house. Here, dried plants hung from the ceiling, jars lined the shelves, some with the usual preserves, and others with special mixes of medicinal leaves unique to Gran. Gran also kept a mortar and pestle there to grind her herbs. That room always smelled slightly musty to Dee, a blend of subtle, spicy scents. Beyond the summer kitchen and the small porch that held their boots and outdoor clothing, across the back to the far side of the garden, was the outhouse—a place Dee had no plans to visit that night. She curled into a small ball beneath her quilt as the wind splashed icy rain against her window.

They didn't have electricity or a telephone. In Price's Corners, tall poles with wires strung between them stretched out to various houses, including Cissy Price's, to provide electric lighting. Cissy was very proud of her new electric lamps. But though the poles crept ever closer, Gran vowed to continue to use kerosene lamps. Some of those poles also carried telephone lines to the police station and to Simpsons' Mercantile, and to Reverend McAllister at the church, among others. Dee remembered the excitement of the wooden poles being put in, and the wires strung, and Mr. Simpson telling her and Mary Ann that someday every home would have electricity and a telephone.

It was funny, Dee thought, how the mind tumbled about aimlessly when all a person wanted was to sleep. It was as if it hoarded every thought collected during the day until she closed her eyes, when it then brought them out to mull over and keep her awake. And they weren't always pleasant thoughts. Was she strange? Billy had said she was, and no doubt other people thought so, too. But they were used to her. What would happen if she left Price's Corners? What if she was somewhere new and it came out that she could *see* or have *feelings*? True, they didn't burn people anymore for being strange, but there were more ways than one to make a person's life miserable. At least she was safe here in Price's Corners.

A flash of lightning lit her room, followed by a crack of thunder. Her mind's eye showed her trees bent beneath the wind, leaves pummelled by rain and tearing free from branches, and Dickson Creek flooding its banks. How many storms had drenched Mary Ann as she lay on the mountain? And that stupid girl, Vivien, kicking up all that emotion in the brown leaves and needles, sending it scattering with the wind to be carried to who knew where, to do unknown harm. A violent death was unexpected, unwanted, and resulted in deep rage at a life cut short. That very anger seeped into the earth, leaving its imprint at the spot where that person died.

Dee had *felt* the remains of a peaceful passing, knowledge of death approaching, and therefore a resignation, if not exactly an acceptance. Peaceful deaths left little residue, usually regret or bitterness or a reluctance to leave the familiar that dissipated quickly. The first time she had felt the imprint of rage left by a violent death was outside a drinking house in Wallen. She'd taken a step and found herself inside a colourless place with two men, fists flying, a blow to one head, and blackness. Gran had tugged on her arm and pulled her out of the scene. "It's a long ago death," Gran told her. "If it happens again, just keep walking through it. Don't stop." Dee made sure to avoid that particular spot whenever she was in town.

She'd heard that the fields in France were impromptu mass graves for soldiers. They'd died young and terribly. Dee could only imagine what horror the land there held, thought it would probably overwhelm her if she ever crossed those fields.

Dee rolled over and remembered the item she'd grabbed from Vivien and stuffed in her pocket. She crawled out of bed, shivering in the cold. In the dark, her hand found her discarded skirt, reached inside the folds of fabric to a pocket, and came out with a small carving, a bird, one of Podge's. She didn't think Vivien had recognized it, as the girl hadn't known Podge that long.

Dee took the carving over to the window and, in the faint light, stroked the wooden feathers. The bird was weathered, with a dark stain on one side where damp had seeped in. It had been outside a long time. But what had it been doing under the tree exactly where the bones had been found? It was true that during the time not spent at the school, Podge wandered the mountain. Perhaps he had dropped it? But beneath the spruce?

She crawled back into bed and put the bird beneath her pillow. All she knew was that she would never tell anyone about it. Come morning, she'd burn the bird in the stove, and that would be the end of it.

With a start, Dee sat straight up. She hadn't *felt* Mary Ann's death under the tree! That was what had been missing. She had stood on the very place where Mary Ann's bones had been found, but there had been no rage, no imprint left in the ground. And, more practically, the tree was old, its roots thick and spreading. Mary Ann had been found by the police in a shallow trench. No one could dig a grave deep enough to hold a body for all those years. No one would try. It could only mean that Mary Ann hadn't been killed beneath the tree. She'd met her death elsewhere. So how had the body come to be found in their secret hiding place? And where *had* she been killed? Dee lay awake long into the night, puzzling over endless questions. Toward dawn the storm eased and, finally, she fell asleep.

Dee woke late the next morning and rushed through her chores. She knew she'd be the last one into the schoolhouse. Leaving late also meant no one had waited to walk with her.

She hurried down the road, mud splashing her buttoned-up boots. As she neared the old Martin house, she saw the young man, back against a tree, staring up at the mountain. Dee glanced over her shoulder to see what up there had caught his interest, and when she turned back, he was gone. She quickly continued on her way, trying to bring him to mind. He was, she decided, more of a boy than a man, and he had been wearing an army uniform. She had seen him so fleetingly, she couldn't recall his hair or eye colour.

As Dee jumped over a puddle, she realized how forlorn the trees looked, last night's wind and rain having stripped them of their leaves. It wouldn't be until snow laced their branches that they would seem less naked.

She hurried into the village, where the streets were empty and quiet. She stopped in front of the police house before crossing the street to the school and saw that the play yard was also deserted. School had started. But before she had a chance to move, Mrs. Carter stepped out her front door, shopping basket in hand. She saw Dee, paused, then pulled the door shut with a bang.

Mrs. Carter was a stout woman, plain of face, with small eyes, one of which drifted off on its own, a lazy eye, Gran called it, leaving the other to focus on a person's face. It was very distracting, Dee found, because she never knew which eye to look at.

Mrs. Carter put on airs because the police house was larger

than most people's homes, and was built of stone cut from the nearby quarry. Behind her and Constable Carter's living quarters was a barred cell in which prisoners could be kept, though it was seldom used. Childless, Mrs. Carter had declared herself head of the Price's Corners Women's Institute and of the Temperance Society for the past three years running. She needed someone to boss around, besides her husband.

"My man was sick the night he was at your place," she finally said.

Dee didn't know what the woman wanted of her. Perhaps she wanted Dee to say that they had poisoned Constable Carter.

"Maybe he ate too much of Gran's cornbread," Dee said. "With jam. He did seem very hungry," she added.

Everyone knew Mrs. Carter couldn't bake worth beans. Her cakes were always the last to be bid on at the church picnic. The men made jokes about how her bread could be used as bricks in a pinch, or how Constable Carter thought army cooking was downright tasty and quite enjoyed the war because of it. All of this was said out of Mrs. Carter's hearing, of course.

"I know what your grandmother and you are. Other people might be scared to cross you, but I'm not." The woman stepped down beside Dee, and her voice dropped to a vicious whisper. "Your grandmother had something to do with Mary Ann Simpson's death. That's what Constable Carter thinks. And he also thinks she had something to do with those other girls, too." Sour breath from bad teeth made Dee draw back.

Mrs. Carter straightened, pulling her shawl about her shoulders. "And I'll be telling Mrs. Simpson that." She pushed past Dee, sweeping her skirts aside so they didn't touch the girl.

School momentarily forgotten, Dee watched Mrs. Carter walk toward the Mercantile. What had the woman meant? What could Gran have possibly had to do with Mary Ann Simpson's death? And what other girls?

Mind churning, Dee turned her feet back down the path on which she'd come. She'd never be able to concentrate in school now. But where to go? Not back home. Gran would want to know why she wasn't in school and would probably just send her right back. Her feet stopped in front of Cissy's house. Ray Price would be gone to the mill and the older children to school.

Dee went around to the backyard. A clothespin in one hand and another in her mouth, Cissy was hanging wet overalls on a line that already held cloth nappies. A toddler played in the dirt at her feet. Seeing Dee, she stopped pinning for a moment, then reached up and pegged a leg of the overalls. As she stretched to reach the line, the gentle swell of her stomach was apparent.

"Would you like a cup of tea?" she asked when she finished. She put the empty laundry basket under one arm, scooped up the toddler, and tucked her under the other.

Dee nodded and followed Cissy inside. The kitchen was moist from the wash Cissy had done, water trickling down the steamy windows. The newest baby stirred in the cradle from the corner of the room but soon settled back into sleep. Dee sat down at the table and pulled the toddler onto her knee to keep her from touching the stove. "Hot," she told her, reminded of the large jar of soothing salve Gran kept for burns, a jar which the mothers in the village emptied regularly.

"Gran's not happy that you're expecting again," Dee said.

Cissy pulled a teapot from the back of the stove, took off the lid, and looked inside. Like most people in the area, she kept tea brewing all day, adding water to the leaves as necessary. "I'm not happy about it either, but that's the way it is."

She set out two cups of tea, adding milk to both. Then she sat down across from Dee. "So why aren't you in school?"

"I met Mrs. Carter," Dee began. To her surprise, tears filled her eyes.

"Oh, well, Mrs. Carter." Cissy leaned forward and patted Dee's hand sympathetically.

Dee had to laugh. Everyone knew Mrs. Carter and her ways. But she quickly sobered. "She said she knew what Gran was. And what I am, too."

"I know what you are," Cissy interrupted. "A lovely, young woman."

"She said some people might be afraid of us, but she wasn't."

Cissy sipped her tea, thinking. Then she set her cup back on its saucer. "You must know that people look at your gran as different."

Dee nodded. Yes, she knew that. But Gran was also the first one they turned to when they had a problem.

"And people sometimes are scared of different, but only because they don't know better. Like Podge. People who don't know him are afraid of him."

"When I was little, I thought everyone was like me," Dee said. "And Gran pretends I'm like everyone else. But I'm not. I'm different and nothing she can do or say will change that."

"I think your gran just wants to spare you some bad times," Cissy said.

Dee went on rapidly, relieved to finally speak her shame aloud. "I sometimes *know* things, things that other people don't usually know, like how someone met his death. I can *feel* it." Her voice dropped to a whisper. "And sometimes I *see* things, like people who are dead."

"It was called 'the sight' in my grandparents' day," Cissy said. "It runs in families, passed down from generation to generation."

"Did my mother have it?" Dee asked.

"I don't think so. At least she never seemed to know ahead of time what was going to happen, and she never mentioned, well, those other things." Cissy shifted in her chair. Talk of ghosts generally did make people uncomfortable, Dee thought, even Cissy.

"People came to Canada bringing their old superstitions and fears with them. Some people think of the sight as witchcraft.

Many years ago, women were burned to death as witches because people feared anything and anyone different.

"Not that I'm saying your gran is a witch," Cissy hastily added. "Your gran has been nothing but good to our family and to all the people in the village. But it's a bit uncanny that she knows beforehand that something is going to happen, and she's very good with healing." Cissy hesitated. "But she shuns church, and some folks say it is because she knows she would be struck dead by God if she ever crossed the threshold."

"She makes me go," Dee said glumly.

Cissy drained her cup. "Reverend McAllister ran afoul of your grandmother with his uncharitable comments about your mother, and your gran isn't very forgiving. But she doesn't want you to carry that burden so she makes you go to church. And people do like to talk."

"You mean Mrs. Carter likes to talk, and others like to listen. There isn't a family around here that Gran hasn't delivered a baby for or made them better when they got ill," Dee said heatedly. "And Mrs. Carter also said Gran had something to do with Mary Ann's death."

"That I know isn't true," Cissy said. "Your gran might have the sight, but she isn't evil, and whatever happened to that girl, it was caused by evil."

The toddler slid off Dee's lap and walked away with unsteady steps.

"And the other girls?" Dee asked.

"What other girls?"

"I thought *you* might know," Dee said. "Mrs. Carter said something about 'other girls,' just like that. I think some others must have disappeared, too."

Cissy got up from the table, poured hot water into a basin, and added a sliver of soap. She began to wash the breakfast dishes, frowning thoughtfully.

"There were a couple of girls who went missing years ago. Long before the war."

"There were? Who were they? What happened to them?" Dee grabbed a cloth and began to dry a bowl. She was surprised to find her hands shaking. Maybe she didn't really want to know.

"Goodness. It's been a while. Let me think. You're what? Fourteen?"

Dee nodded.

"The first one I know of was that girl from Wallen. That would have been sixteen years ago. People thought she'd wandered up the mountain and got lost. Your mama and I were fourteen at the time. I remember my dad and your grandpa helping with the search."

"And they didn't find her?" Dee asked.

"No. Nothing of her at all. Not even a piece of clothing.

"And then Mr. Richmond, who owns the mill. His daughter went missing the year after that. She was a really pretty girl.

Poor Mr. Richmond, he doted on her. He had three sons and
she was his only daughter. I would sit in church envying her
clothes, which I guess isn't a very churchly thing to do," Cissy
admitted.

"I remember hearing about her," Dee said. "Didn't she
drown?"

"Yes. It turned out not to be a mystery after all. Her dress
was found a year later by Podge, at the bottom of Brewsters'
Falls."

Podge. Dee's stomach lurched as she remembered the
wooden bird still under her pillow. She'd forgotten to burn it.

"It was thought that she must have taken a misstep and
fallen off the cliffs—they are so steep right there—and
drowned in the pool at the bottom and been dragged down-
stream. After they found that dress they looked for a while,
but never found her body."

"But it is pretty sure she drowned?"

"Well, yes. What with her dress being found at the falls
and all." Cissy scrubbed a pot. "Of course, everyone wondered
why she was up the mountain in the first place. Especially
in her best dress. She wasn't an active girl. Not one for taking walks and the like. It was strange. And now that I think
about it, I do remember there was a girl from the other side
of the mountain. We didn't know her, but I remember talk
in town of her disappearing. That would have been in . . ."

Cissy stopped, thinking. "I guess in 1912. I never did hear what happened to her."

"And then Mary Ann disappeared," Dee said.

"Yes, four years ago, 1915, just after the start of the war," Cissy said. "Poor Mrs. Simpson. I think in her heart of hearts she thought Mary Ann had run away and would one day come back."

Dee carefully put the dried bowl on the table. She couldn't seem to catch her breath. "That's a lot of girls gone missing," she said.

Cissy shrugged. "People go missing all the time, get lost in the woods, or a foolish girl follows a man and gets her heart broken and is too ashamed to come home. It's a tragedy but it does happen." Cissy turned around and dried her hands. "I wouldn't put a lot of store in what Mrs. Carter says. She does love to hear herself speak."

The baby whimpered in the cradle, then set up a demanding howl. Cissy picked him up, sat down, and unbuttoned the front of her dress. "This one falls asleep before he's finished eating, then wakes up hungry again a few minutes later."

Dee sat back down at the table across from her. "Cissy, have you ever heard from Mama? Since she left, I mean."

Cissy stroked the baby's fine hair. "No. But your mama wasn't really one for writing. She hated school." She smiled. "Besides, if she wrote to anyone, it would be you and your gran."

"She didn't disappear like those others?"

"Good heavens, no. Didn't you get that seashell from her?"

Dee nodded.

"Well, there you go, then. She's fine or you would have heard. Bad news always has a way of coming home."

Dee wanted to believe Cissy. She really did, but now that the doubt had been planted, she couldn't rid herself of it.

She had just one last question for Cissy. One she'd wanted to ask for a long time, yet at each opportunity lost her nerve. But today she needed to ask it. Anxiously, she got up and wandered around the kitchen, handling a cup, then a dish, building up her courage. One part of her dreaded hearing the answer, while another needed to know.

Cissy cooed to the baby. "Out with it, Dee. You're making me dizzy going around and around my kitchen. What's bothering you?"

Dee took a deep breath. "I was wondering—do you know who my father is?"

Cissy tilted her head to one side, studying Dee for a long moment. Finally she spoke. "No. Your mama never even told me that she had a beau. She shared everything with me, just like you do with Clooey, so it came as a real surprise to me when I heard she was expecting. The last time I saw your mama, we went up the mountain a little ways for a walk. It was a lovely evening, but the flies were biting. They nearly drove me crazy.

'Come home with me,' I said to her. But your mama, she said the evening was so beautiful it was like a gift, and she wanted to enjoy it a little longer. I went home, and your mama stayed. And that was the last time I saw her. After that, your gran kept her in all the time. She never let me see her. I would go over to the house, but your gran would block the doorway and say that your mama wasn't feeling well and to come back later. After a while, I stopped going." Cissy smiled. "I didn't even know she was expecting until I heard that she had a beautiful baby girl, and then right after your birth, your mother left. She surprised me by doing that, too. It didn't seem in her nature to leave her baby." Cissy shrugged. "Does it matter so very much? You know who you are."

"I only know half of who I am."

"But it's a good half," Cissy said gently.

CHAPTER EIGHT

Dee stood in the laneway outside Cissy's house, wondering what to do next. The morning was just half over, so she could return to school, but having to explain to Miss Hamilton why she was late wasn't very appealing. Neither was going home to Gran and chores. Her eyes strayed to the mountain. That was where she needed to be. Up there. Alone. Looking out over the world. That never failed to make her problems seem smaller. She buttoned her wool coat to the neck against the cold wind and made her way back down the road.

As she neared the old Martin place, she saw that the young man was back, this time standing in the middle of the road and, as before, his gaze was fixed on the mountain.

"Hello," she said.

He swivelled his head to look at her and frowned, as if puzzled to see her. Probably wondering why she wasn't in school, Dee thought. He had the look of Vivien about him, though his face had sharper, more masculine, planes, and his eyes were a deep blue, rather than the odd pale shade of the girl's. He did, though, have the same blond hair as his sister beneath his soldier's cap. Dee unexpectedly found herself flustered.

"I guess you're glad Billy's father finished your roof before the rain," she said. It was the only thing she could think of to say.

"Rain?" he said. He seemed dazed.

"The rain. Last night." Dee pointed to a large puddle. "You would have been very wet if your roof wasn't fixed."

"Oh. Yes, I guess so," he replied.

"I'm Dee." She held out her hand, but the boy had turned his eyes back to the mountain and didn't notice, so Dee let her hand drop.

"Clarence," he said briefly.

"Are you Vivien's brother?"

"Yes." He looked back at her.

Dee didn't know when she'd seen eyes so blue, or so filled with pain.

"I've seen you next door," Clarence said.

"My grandmother and I live there. You must have just got back from overseas." She gestured toward his uniform.

"Yes." He looked at the house. "It took me a while to find them."

"You didn't know they had moved?" Dee asked.

His glance shifted from the house to Dee to the mountain. He couldn't seem to focus on one thing. Jittery. The war had done a lot of damage to people, to body and mind, Gran said.

Reminded of Gran, Dee glanced at the house. All quiet, but Gran could step out at any moment and see Dee. She took a step away. "Bye," she said.

"Are you going up there?" Clarence asked.

"Yes, I am," Dee replied. She hesitated. She really wanted to be on her own, and something about this boy made her shy, unsure of herself. But he looked so lost standing there. "Do you want to come with me? I can show you some of the paths so you can find your own way another time." She felt very forward inviting this stranger to come with her. One part of her wondered if it was safe, but she didn't get any bad *feeling* from him. She was just all nerves from Cissy's talk of missing girls. She had nothing to be afraid of. Those girls had all disappeared a long time ago. And Mary Ann? Well, this boy wasn't even around when she had gone missing, so it had nothing to do with him.

The boy nodded and fell into step beside her. He seemed lost in his own thoughts, so Dee decided conversation wasn't called for. She hurried past her house, crossed over the split in the road and the bridge, and led the way up the mountainside.

A few minutes later, she realized she didn't hear footsteps behind her and turned around, fearing she'd lost him. But he was climbing steadily behind her.

At one point, on a steep part of the trail, Dee's hard-soled boots slipped on shale and she put a hand down to steady herself. Regaining her balance, she looked up to see a man standing to the right of the path, a silver shimmering aura outlining him. She gave him a quick nod and he disappeared. Sometimes nothing more was required by the dead than acknowledgement. Then, remembering Clarence behind her, she glanced over her shoulder to see if he'd seen her nod at thin air and was surprised to see that he was staring at the exact spot where the man had stood. It shook her momentarily, but she straightened and continued climbing. It was probably just by chance that Clarence was looking at that particular spot, she told herself.

After a half-hour's steady climb, Dee pushed her way through thick grape vines and a tangle of underbrush and onto a flat rock shelf. In summer it was nearly impossible to get through the stinging nettles and thorns blocking the way. But last night's rain and wind had stripped many of the nettles' leaves and wilted others, making the passage easier. She still avoided the thorns, though. The cold didn't make them any less sharp.

The rock shelf jutted out from the mountainside, overlooking the valley and beyond. A single pine tree sprang from a crack that split the stone, its trunk precariously overhanging the edge, roots doggedly clinging to whatever meagre soil it could find. For years it had stubbornly hung on while wind tore at it, rain drenched it, and snow bowed it branches. Defiant. She smiled. Just like her.

There were higher areas farther up the mountain with better views, but this one was Dee's favourite because the shelf had a boulder weathered into the shape of a stone chair. She'd never brought anyone up here, not even Clooey. She'd kept the place a secret, needing it for herself. Why then had she brought Clarence? As he pushed out from the brush behind her, Dee felt her shyness return. What if he thought the "chair" was dumb? What if he thought she was just some stupid girl? He had, after all, been across the Atlantic Ocean and seen other places much nicer than this, probably met much smarter girls, too.

He stood on the lip of the shelf, toes hanging in the air, making Dee nervous, though he didn't look worried about the sheer drop before him. "It's beautiful."

His pleasure in the view freed Dee's tongue. "And you see how this is like a chair? You can sit right in it. I come up here a lot. Sometimes I bring a book to read and I sit in this chair because it is so comfortable. But mostly I just like looking out." She was talking too fast and too much. She wanted to say his name, but it stuck on her tongue. It felt forward calling him by his first name. It was okay with Billy, but she'd known him all her life.

He turned to see, and nodded. "It looks like a fine place to sit and read."

Dee joined him at the shelf's edge, but kept her feet firmly planted on rock. It was a heavy day, the air damp from the previous night's rain. It had intensified the odour of rotting leaves, wet dirt, and faraway wood smoke. Patchy blue sky showed where the clouds had been torn apart.

Wind whipped Dee's navy serge skirt tight around her legs and blew her hair wildly about her face. She felt pure joy sweep over her. "It's like I can see the entire world from up here," she shouted over the wind.

Directly below them were spindly pines, maple trees, and white-trunked birches. Farther away they could see the sliver of silver river that sliced through the valley, swollen and running fast from yesterday's downpour. Beyond it, contrasting starkly with the wildness of the mountain slopes, were orderly farm fields, harvested now, the brown soil turned and prepared for winter. Thin threads of smoke twisted away from miniature house chimneys. Dee felt a pang of guilt when she looked toward Price's Corners and the schoolhouse, but she resolutely turned her eyes skyward to where a hawk circled.

The boy tilted his head, listening. "Is there a waterfall nearby?"

Dee pointed to her left. "Over there is the biggest one. There are lots of small ones, too. I can show them to you sometime if you like," she offered tentatively. Did she seem too eager? For some reason, she wanted him to have a good opinion of her.

"I'd like that," he said. "You can see the horizon curve," he added.

"I know," Dee said. "Sometimes when I look out, I lose my balance. The horizon reminds me that the earth is round and moving all the time." She immediately wished she'd not shared that with him. Her tongue was getting ahead of her brain, babbling such nonsense.

"I can see how that would happen," Clarence said solemnly.

Again, Dee felt grateful that he hadn't made fun of her. So grateful that she grinned widely. Billy, well, he would have just laughed at her, told her she was fanciful, that all girls were fanciful, because his ma said so.

Clarence smiled hesitantly in return, then pointed. "What's that town over there? Where the church steeple is."

"Wallen," Dee replied. "It's the biggest town around here. You must have got off the train there to come to Price's Corners."

"Yes. I must have," the boy echoed, but without certainty. "Sorry, sometimes I forget things. I guess it's from the war."

Dee nodded and pointed to a large building with a water wheel on the river, set halfway between Price's Corners and Wallen. "That's Mr. Richard's woollen mill. You might be able to find work there. He likes to hire returning soldiers. Though, now that he's not making blankets for the army, it's not as busy."

"That's good of him. There's not much work around for those soldiers coming home," Clarence said. The blue of his eyes deepened with anger. "People seem to resent the fact we came back at all. They resent that the soldiers need jobs and help. I saw a newspaper the other day that called the war 'an international unpleasantness.' I guess that makes it easier for people. It's easier to think someone lost a leg in *an international unpleasantness* rather than in a war. You don't owe that someone quite so much when it's an *unpleasantness.*" He spat out his bitterness.

"But we've been buying Victory bonds throughout the war. We still are. Prime Minister Borden, he tells us to keep buying them even though the war is over so that we can help retrain soldiers to get new jobs," Dee told him.

Clarence turned back to look out over the fields and threw a hand out toward the mill. "They can talk about retraining all they want," he said. "But that can't grow a man another arm or leg, or give him new eyes. Who'll hire someone with half a face?"

Dee didn't know what to say. She sat down on the shelf and ran her fingers over the cold stone curves of a long-dead beetle, its body captured in the rock for all of time. Here was a life lived long before her own. What would she look like thousands and thousands of years from now? Dust probably, unless she was captured in stone. Then maybe there would be a surprised look on her face, death having caught her unawares; or perhaps there would be a smile on her lips.

"Sorry," the boy said after a moment. His shoulders sagged with weariness, now that the rage was gone. "My folks always did tell me to get off my soapbox. I didn't mean to upset you."

"You didn't upset me. I don't get upset easily."

He crouched beside her and examined the stone. "Fossils."

Fingers moving over the rock, Dee said, "I can't believe all the life caught inside this stone. You can see wings, spines, scales." She pointed to a larger imprint. "This one looks like it might have been a shell. See the coils? And these . . ." She traced a feathery spray embedded in rock. "This must have been a plant, like a fern. And there are a lot of fish skeletons. Miss Hamilton, our teacher, says that this area was once a great sea millions of years ago. Can you imagine all this under water? She says as plants and creatures died, they were compressed into sand, which over millions of years became stone. Then a million years of water and wind wore away the stone, uncovering the fossils." Dee tried, but she couldn't imagine a million years.

"I wonder if that's what they'll find in France a million years from now, but human remains, not bugs," Clarence mused.

Just then, a squirrel leapt into the pine tree and scolded them loudly. Clarence started, jumped up, but seeing no threat, settled back down again.

"Look at the layers of rock across there." He pointed to an exposed part of the rock face opposite them. "That's like staring at years and years gone by. Compared with all that, all that time needed to build up this mountain, why, we're just a flash in the pan."

Dee felt an urge to tell Clarence about Mary Ann. She wanted to say to this young man: my friend, a girl I knew really well, was found dead up here a week ago. Well, her bones were found. Not in rock, but beneath a pine tree. She wasn't sure why she wanted to tell him. Maybe so he'd know that she understood about death. Or maybe she just needed to share Mary Ann with someone. But she didn't. Instead she said, "I should go home."

"I didn't upset you with all my talk, did I?" Clarence asked. He seemed genuinely concerned. "I didn't mean to. It's just that there's been no one to talk to since I got back . . ." His voice trailed off.

"I don't mind your talking," Dee said. "It's just that my Gran will be wondering where I am."

Clarence smiled and turned back to look out at the view again. "I think I'll stay a while. If that's fine with you, this being your special place," he added.

"You can come here any time you like," Dee told him.

And she meant it, she realized, as her boots skidded down the mountain. It was lovely to have something special of your own, but sharing it was like, well, giving a gift. It left you warm all over. And Clarence? She had the feeling that he understood exactly what that gift was worth.

CHAPTER NINE

From the middle of the footbridge, Dee saw automobiles sitting outside her house. Chief O'Brien and Dr. Hughes again. Had something happened to Gran? She ran the rest of the way home, arriving out of breath to find Clooey at the gate, nervously twisting a handkerchief in her hand.

"You weren't at school," Clooey said. "Ma wanted me to come home with you and get some medicine for Mister. But you weren't at school so I had to come myself."

"I'm sorry, Clooey. I was up the mountain. I'll tell you all about it later," Dee promised. She hadn't realized that she'd been up the mountain so long that school was out already.

"I didn't want to go in and see your gran with them in there." Clooey nodded toward the automobiles. "Especially Dr. Hughes. He wants Mister to go to hospital, but Ma says she'll take care of him at home because we don't have the money."

"I'll take you in," said Dee. She grabbed Clooey's arm and started to steer the girl through the gate when she glanced over her shoulder and saw Vivien and Billy standing beneath a tree, talking. Or rather, Billy was talking. Vivien was smiling absently and looking off into the distance, clearly not listening, but that didn't seem to bother Billy at all.

"The lovebirds," Clooey said, following Dee's glance. "Everyone at school is talking about them. Some of the girls said you weren't at school because you were mad at Billy for dropping you."

"For dropping me? I spurned him!" Dee marched up the path to the house. "I have no plans to be married. Especially to the likes of Billy Haynes. Besides, you and I have plans to go to Wallen next year to school."

Clooey frowned as Dee pulled her into the kitchen, but said nothing.

Dr. Hughes and Chief O'Brien sat at the table. Constable Carter, with his notebook, sat in a chair near the door. Gran stood with her back to the stove, arms crossed. This wasn't a friendly visit: there were no coffee cups or plates of cornbread on the table. Obviously, Gran didn't feel the need to offer refreshment. By the wary look on Constable Carter's clean-shaven face, he wouldn't have accepted it anyway.

"Girls," Chief O'Brien said. He half rose and nodded. Dr. Hughes stayed seated, though his hand strayed to his moustache, smoothing first one end, then the other.

Clooey stopped in the doorway, afraid to go into the kitchen. "Mrs. Vale, Ma sent me for some medicine for Mister. His chest is bad again," she whispered nervously.

Dee's grandmother got up and went into the summer kitchen. A few minutes later she returned with two small paper packages. She held one out to Clooey. "This will help ease the cough, and this one . . ." She held out the second parcel. "Tell your ma to make it into a strong tea before bedtime to help him sleep. Now mind you don't get them mixed up."

Clooey took a package in each hand. "I won't, Mrs. Vale. Ma says she'll settle up with you later."

Gran nodded. "And tell your mother to try some steam. It might help rest the lungs."

Dr. Hughes's fingers drummed on the table. Annoyed, Dee knew, that Gran was dispensing her medicine, while he, a real doctor with real medicine, sat right there in the kitchen. Gran ignored him.

Dee went with Clooey to the front door. "I'll see you tomorrow at school and we'll set those girls straight about those lovebirds." She and Clooey exchanged grins and Dee shut the door.

"I understand you weren't in school today," Gran said.

"Sorry," Dee said quickly. Might as well get it over with. "I was up the mountain." She stopped. How to explain that Mrs. Carter had upset her when Constable Carter sat right there? "Thinking things over," she finished weakly.

Gran fixed a look on Dee. "If you weren't planning on going to school, there was lots of work for you here, rather than you wasting your time wandering about," she said.

Dee nodded.

Chief O'Brien cleared his throat. "We have some more information about Mary Ann Simpson and a few more questions for you both."

"My granddaughter doesn't know anything about this matter. There is nothing she can tell you. She'd be better off out doing her chores."

"Yes, well, as she's here, I'd like to talk to her," he said. "First of all, Dr. Hughes here has finished examining the bones, and it appears that Mary Ann was in the—" he paused, searching for the correct words, "—the family way. Dr. Hughes found smaller bones among those of Mary Ann. At first we thought they might be animal, but . . ." His voice trailed off.

"Did you know she was expecting?" Dr. Hughes asked.

"Yes," Gran replied.

Dee looked at her, surprised. Gran had never said anything about that to her.

"Did she come to you?" Chief O'Brien asked. "Looking for something to—" His face went red. He shifted uncomfortably in his chair. "Well, help her?" he finished. "With her problem, if you get my meaning."

"I get your meaning, and no, I don't help women with unwanted pregnancies." Gran spoke bluntly. "I remind women that they have a tongue in their heads and to speak up to their husbands, and I tell the young ones to not get into situations they can't handle, but if the *problem* does occur, well, that's the way it is and I tell them they have to accept it. I let the unmarried ones know there are places they can go away to, to have their babies, and no one would be the wiser when they returned from a holiday."

Constable Carter snorted at that. Dee knew what he was thinking. The way tongues wagged in Price's Corners, very few people wouldn't know why a girl went away on a "holiday."

Gran turned a sour look on the constable and his face reddened. He bent over his notebook and scribbled.

"I see a lot of women in the family way, and I saw Mary Ann in town shortly before she disappeared, and I knew she was expecting," Dee's grandmother went on. "I doubt the girl knew herself. I did wonder if her parents had put that story around about her disappearing because they had sent her away, but their grief was too real. I have no idea who the father was," she added, anticipating Chief O'Brien's next question.

Dr. Hughes turned to Dee. "Are you sure you don't know who was courting Mary Ann?"

"Who gave her the ring?" Constable Carter suddenly said from his corner. "You were with her all the time. She must have told you."

From near the stove, a shadow detached itself from the others, towering up to the ceiling, a pillar of dark, like the one Dee had seen on the bridge when Mary Ann's bones were brought down. Dee could sense it waiting, watching, anxious to hear what she would say. She stared at the men. Couldn't they see it? Couldn't they feel the heat? Couldn't they smell the acrid, burning stench of it?

"She was only ten, a little girl," Gran answered for her. She sat down beside Dee. "She would have no idea about that sort of thing."

"She might have seen something, or Mary Ann might have said something that didn't make sense at the time but does now. She needs to speak for herself. You put yourself forward too much, Madam!" Dr. Hughes leaned forward and slapped the table with his open palm, angry that Gran had interrupted.

Chief O'Brien put a steadying hand on the doctor's arm.

"There's a girl dead here," Dr. Hughes began, then he sat back, smoothing his moustache as he fought to gain control.

Dee fixed her eyes on the doctor's fingers; anything rather than look at that churning pillar of black.

She finally managed to work her tongue. "No. I can't think of anything. Just that she said she was engaged and showed me the ring."

"And you never asked who the lucky man was?" Chief O'Brien shot a warning glance at Dee's grandmother.

"No," Dee said.

Should she say anything about her suspicions that the body hadn't been buried under the tree? A quick glance at the black column stilled her tongue. The sooner the men left, the sooner the shadow would, too.

Chief O'Brien looked at Gran. "Mrs. Vale, people say you have the uncanny ability to know things that others don't."

The shadow oozed down the wall and across the floor toward the table. Dee wanted to shriek, to warn Gran and the men, but she knew that if she opened her mouth the black would flow down her throat, poisoning her before any words could leave her mouth. She clamped her teeth together.

"Now, I don't believe in those superstitions myself, but I have to ask. Do you know how Mary Ann died? Do you know anything?" Chief O'Brien pulled out a handkerchief and mopped his sweating forehead.

"You don't need anyone who supposedly *knows* things to tell you she was murdered. But I don't know how she died. Or at whose hand."

Dee barely heard her grandmother's words. Frozen with horror, she watched the darkness reach her chair, then her feet, and crawl up her legs, burning, burning. She opened her mouth to scream but only a moan escaped her lips. Dots crowded her vision. She was dying. A hand suddenly gripped hers under the table and squeezed hard, fighting to free Dee of the dark shadow. Gran. A battle was taking place between her grandmother and the shadow, a battle for Dee. She clung to the hand, hoping her gran would win.

"As Constable Carter told you the last time we were here . . ."

The constable tried to make himself smaller in his chair. Obviously, he had heard from his superior about his indiscretion.

"Mary Ann's skull was broken," Chief O'Brien went on. "At first we thought she'd taken a fall, but the break is too high up on the head. It was a blow that killed her; a hard blow by someone's hand." He hesitated. "But Dr. Hughes has since discovered nicks on the bones that he attributes to knife wounds; she was also stabbed," he ended bluntly.

"I'm sorry she met such a fearful death, but I don't know anything about it," Gran told him.

Abruptly, the constriction in Dee's chest lessened as the shadow slowly retreated across the kitchen floor toward the stove. She pulled in a shuddering breath.

"Sorry," Chief O'Brien said. "I didn't mean to upset Dee. These are hard things for tender ears to hear."

Gran loosened Dee's hand and stood up. "As I said before, a young death is always an unnatural death. And now, I think Dee has had enough questions for one day."

Chief O'Brien slowly pushed back his chair, preparing to leave. As he stood, he glanced over at the front door, and his eyes widened. Dee also turned, in time to see a girl slip out of the house. Vivien! How long had she been there? And what had she heard?

"Well, she's a right nosy little miss," Constable Carter said. "Sneaking around like that, she just might find herself in trouble like those other girls."

"That's enough, Constable," Chief O'Brien chided him. He walked heavily to the door, followed by Dr. Hughes and a now subdued constable. "The Simpsons are burying their girl the day after tomorrow," he said. "At least they now have a body to put to rest. It should help them some."

He opened the door, waited for the others to go through, then stood and stared through the late afternoon gloom to the mountain. "You're in a lonesome spot here, Mrs. Vale. Other than those new folks next door, there's no one around. Feelings are running high in town. People are spreading malicious gossip." He threw an unfriendly grimace at Constable Carter's back. Everyone knew who was spreading the gossip.

"You might want to keep close to home for a few days. Watch yourself after dark."

"I can take care of myself and my own," Gran said.

Chief O'Brien sized her up for a moment, nodded, and left.

CHAPTER TEN

Dee remained seated at the kitchen table, knowing her trembling legs would never support her weight. Nothing remained now of the black pillar.

"What was that?" she asked shakily.

Her grandmother didn't answer but busied herself putting more wood in the stove and ladling water into the kettle. Then she went into the summer kitchen, returning with a jar in hand. She opened it and spooned a bit of its contents into a cup.

"Gran!" Dee exclaimed.

"First I'm making a tea to steady you. Then we'll talk," Gran promised.

Shakily, Dee unrolled a stocking and examined her bare leg. So intense had been the black shadow's heat, she expected to see blisters or angry red burns. There was nothing.

The kettle boiled, and a few minutes later her grandmother placed a steaming cup of tea in front of her. "Drink that. It'll help with the shock. Those men shouldn't come here upsetting you."

Dee took a sip. "Gran, you know it wasn't the men. It was that—that black—that—stink and burning." No fully formed sentence would come to Dee's mind to describe the terrifying presence.

She drank her tea and took a deep breath. "And don't tell me it was my imagination. I didn't imagine *that*. I know you felt it, too. It's the same thing that was on the bridge the day they brought Mary Ann's bones down."

Her grandmother sank into the chair recently occupied by the chief. "Evil. It was evil. What you saw was its true form. I can't see it," she added. "I can only sense when it's near." She paused, then said, "Granddaughter, what does it look like?"

Dee shuddered. "It's a black pillar, tall and thin, and all the time it moves inside, swirling, and . . ." Dee's voice shook. "And in the black I think I see faces; terrible, screaming faces."

Gran bent her head, but not before Dee saw the fear that darkened her grandmother's eyes. Never had she seen her grandmother frightened before, and that started Dee's heart pounding again.

"Drink your tea."

Dee obediently picked up her cup. "Was it one of them? One of the men?"

Her grandmother shook her head, though she didn't raise it. "I don't know. Perhaps, though I hate to think that. Then again, it might just have attached itself to them, trying to find out what they know. Evil has a way of disguising itself. Like a parasite or worm, it gets inside a person and lives off them and makes that person do terrible things, while on the outside they look all clean and pure. I just can't say. I've only felt it that strong once before."

"When?" Dee asked.

"I've tried so hard to keep you safe." Gran didn't appear to hear her.

"Safe from what? Gran, you have to tell me what is happening," Dee said impatiently. "I'm not a child any longer. I need to know these things."

"It's difficult to explain, Granddaughter." Gran raised her head.

"Gran, I know that I'm different. I know I'm not like other people. I *see* things that others don't see; like dead people. What did you think? That if you just ignored the fact I was different, it would go away? Because it's not going away. Cissy says it's called 'the sight' and it runs in families." She banged her cup down on the table and waited.

"My own granny had it back in Scotland," Gran said unexpectedly. "It's like a family having a talent for singing, or a father passing down a carpentry skill. But this particular skill isn't acceptable. It scares people. They think we're drawing on dark forces. That we're working with the devil to harm them, ruin their crops, or speed their passing if we take a dislike to them. All foolishness, of course. When I started to display some of the same skill, that's when my ma and da brought the family to Canada. Maybe they thought I'd lose it on the ocean, or it wouldn't work here."

"Why didn't you ever tell me before?" Dee asked. "Do you know how scared and alone I've felt?"

"I thought if I didn't tell you about it, you'd be safe. Even now, with telephones and electricity and automobiles, they don't look kindly upon people with the sight."

"Like Mrs. Carter," Dee said.

"You had a run-in with Mrs. Carter?" Gran asked.

"On my way to school this morning. That's why I was truant. She said you and I were witches and responsible for Constable Carter's getting sick after he was here."

Gran sniffed. "It was his own greed that did that, or his wife's cooking."

"She also said you were responsible for Mary Ann's death. And for the other girls who went missing. It upset me, her saying such awful things. I didn't know what she meant. So I went to Cissy's, and she told me about how those other girls disappeared years ago. I didn't want to go back to school after that, so I went up the mountain to think." Dee stopped there, reluctant to say anything about Clarence accompanying her. Best one offence at a time.

Gran clicked her tongue. "Women like Mrs. Carter cause

more harm with their tongues than any person did with the sight. She's a malicious gossip."

"So, are we evil? Is that why it was here in our house?" Dee asked. She may as well get all the questions out while Gran was willing to answer them.

"No. There is nothing evil about you. Or at least no more so than the ordinary child." Gran raised her grey-haired head and smiled wryly. "Evil is probably around us every day. We, you and I, just have the ability to sense these things more than other folk. I think today it felt threatened. That's why it showed itself. You must be very, very careful." Gran put an age-freckled hand over Dee's.

Dee mulled that over for a bit, then asked, "Did Grandpa know you had the sight?"

"Yes, of course he did. I was the one who told him he was going to marry me. It didn't bother him."

"And Mama?"

Gran got up and went to the long table beneath the window, her back turned to Dee. "No, I don't believe she did. It sometimes skips a generation. Perhaps if she had . . ."

"If she had—what?"

Her grandmother busied herself wrapping up half a loaf of bread and some bacon in a cloth. She added a square of butter.

"Do you *know* where Mama is?" Dee asked, angry that her grandmother had stopped talking. Why, whenever she wanted to know something about her mother, did her grandmother brush her off?

"We don't get to pick and choose what we *know* or *see,*" Gran replied. "What we do with it. *That* we do get to choose."

"But is that why she went away?" Dee persisted. "Because of the way we are? Because of the way I am? Was she afraid of me?"

Her grandmother went into the backroom and returned with a cabbage.

"Your mother loved you." Gran handed the cabbage and parcel to Dee, then added a small paper package of tea leaves. "Run these over to next door. The mother is doing poorly. This might help, though I expect it will take more than a calming tea to erase her grief. Still, those children have to eat. Vivien looked like she was half starving." Gran shook her head. "I never thought I'd say this, but I agree with Constable Carter that that girl is going to get herself into trouble."

So that was it! Her grandmother wasn't going to answer any more questions. Fuming, Dee headed out the door. "Granddaughter!" Gran's voice followed her. "Don't dawdle. Be back before dark. You need to take extra care now."

Dee stomped across the yard toward the line of evergreens that separated the two properties. She knew why Mama had left Price's Corners. Because Gran had driven her away. Gran, who wouldn't answer her questions. Gran with her secrets. Or, had her mother left because she feared her newborn daughter would be different, too?

A fog had risen from the moist ground to wrap around the trunks of the trees that divided the two properties. Water softly dripped from the branches, whispering the trees' secrets. Dee's legs shook slightly as she contemplated the dark shadows beneath the boughs, then chided herself for her cowardice and ducked under them. Still, she held her breath, only letting it out when she pushed safely through to the other side. Carefully, she picked her way in the twilight through the stone-studded field to the far side where the old Martin house stood.

She knocked on the door, which was opened immediately by one of the boys. "It's Dee," he called over his shoulder. He shut the door in her face.

Surprised, Dee stood there a moment. She had just made up her mind to leave the goods on the steps and go home when the door opened again, this time by Vivien.

"What do you want?" she asked bluntly, though her voice wasn't unfriendly, just disinterested.

"Gran thought your mother might like these." Dee held out the packages and head of cabbage.

"Who is it?" a woman's voice called weakly from inside the house.

Vivien turned her head toward the dark interior. "Dee Vale from next door." She turned back. "You may as well come in."

Dee had to admit to a certain curiosity as she stepped inside the house. First thing she did was look up. Sure enough, the roof was fixed. As her eyes adjusted to the room's gloom, she saw a woman sitting in a chair near the stove, her face gaunt, her hair hanging in strings about her shoulders, defeated. Life had beaten her down. Then Dee realized she was standing there like a dolt, staring rudely. She quickly held out the packages and cabbage again. "Gran thought you might have some use for these. We had a bumper crop of cabbages. We also have some sewing to be done when you're feeling up to it."

That last she had just made up on the spot. They were well able to do their own sewing, she and Gran, but one didn't just give charity. It took away a person's pride. Gran had taught her that. Vivien's mother might feel better taking the food if she thought some stitching would repay them.

"And Gran sent you some tea leaves, for headaches and such." Except this woman looked like she needed more than tea leaves to get her back on her feet.

The room was cool and damp, and the children sat listlessly in a row on a bench in front of an open fire. Smoke drifted into the room, and Dee suspected that the chimney was partially blocked. Perhaps she should say something to Clarence. She stole a quick glance around the room but didn't see him.

"There's a loaf of bread here, too, some butter, and bacon," Dee added.

Mac, who had answered the door, jumped forward and with a cry pulled the teacloth from the food. The children wrestled the loaf among themselves, tearing off chunks and stuffing them in their mouths. The butter was ignored until Esther scooped a bit with her finger and began to eat it, without the bread. Vivian's mother sighed and laid her head back on the chair, saying nothing about her children's manners.

Dee tried not to look horrified, tried to look as if it was perfectly normal that the children act like a pack of wild dogs.

"I need it dark because the light hurts my head," Vivien's mother said, as if reading Dee's mind. "Thank your grandmother for me. Tell her I'll get to that sewing in a day or two." She closed her eyes as if the effort of those few sentences had worn her out.

Dee felt slightly dizzy from the lack of light and air in the room. She'd already had enough difficulty breathing this evening without the scent of unwashed bodies and clothing to contend with. The closeness of the room pressed down on her.

"I'd better go. Gran wants me straight back," Dee said.

Vivien followed Dee out to the porch. "Why were those men asking you about that girl?"

"I used to be her friend," Dee said. "And you shouldn't be sneaking into people's houses without being invited," Dee added.

Vivien merely shrugged.

Anxious to escape the brooding house, Dee ran across the field, not worrying about stones and stumbling, just wanting to get home. She sucked in great gulps of cold air, feeling guilty that she didn't have to live in that house, live with the gloom, the poverty, the stink, and the overwhelming grief residing there. This too, she realized, was a type of darkness; a different sort than the one that had invaded her own home, but darkness nonetheless. And, perhaps, a breeding ground for the other? The thought sprang unbidden into her mind.

Thoughts of the black pillar spurred Dee to run even faster, afraid she'd be caught halfway home and pulled into that dark swirl, become one of those terrified faces that screamed within it, and never be able to leave.

The mist had crept up into the topmost branches of the pines now, completely shrouding the trees. Dee burst through them, not caring that boughs snagged her hair and slapped her arms and legs. She nearly wept with relief to see the yellow light from her kitchen window piercing the mist.

CHAPTER ELEVEN

It was cold and bleak the morning of Mary Ann's burial; the town was clothed in a white dripping mist, as it had been for the past two days. Dee couldn't see the mountain, but she felt it looming above her, looming over Price's Corners. Others, she saw, felt it, too. The mourners, coats pulled tight against the damp, huddled in the graveyard around the waiting hole in the earth, faces long and tongues subdued. They stared at black-turned dirt, the simple wooden coffin, at the minister, or the stone church—anywhere but at each other.

Most of the town had turned out for the service, some to grieve with Mr. and Mrs. Simpson, some because they fed on others' sadness, and some because of the excitement; after all, not many people could say they'd been to the funeral of a murdered girl.

Dee raised her eyes from the dark hole to see Chief O'Brien, Dr. Hughes, and Mrs. Hughes standing a little apart from the mourners. Tiny Mrs. Hughes was dressed in a stylish cloth coat, with a lavish fur stole thrown over her shoulders;

her gloved hand rested in the crook of her husband's arm. That wrap alone, Dee thought, should have given the doctor's wife substance, but instead she appeared frail; a whiff of smoke easily dispersed. It was said that she suffered from melancholia and required a great deal of rest, so was seldom seen. A sign of good breeding, Dee had once overheard Mrs. Carter say, to be stricken with melancholia. She had then gone on to declare that she sometimes suffered from bouts of it herself but, for Constable Carter's sake, made herself go on. She also liked to point out that like her and the constable, Dr. and Mrs. Hughes were not blessed with children, as if the inability to bear offspring was yet another sign of good breeding.

Clooey, black hair flattened by the damp, stood with her mother directly across from Dee. She looked up once, gave Dee a fleeting smile, then quickly bowed her head. Mister, with the burned lungs, was unable to come. Podge and his mother stood behind Clooey, Podge sniffling and wiping his nose with his sleeve, upset by the grave and the sorrow.

Mr. Forgetti had come by himself, Maggie kept home by the new baby. He stood near the cemetery's iron fence, aware that he was an outsider in Prices' Corners despite the thirteen years he'd lived nearby.

Another who had come alone was Mr. Richmond, owner of the mill. His wife had died the previous year. In formal black dress, tall silk hat in hand and head bare to the elements, he was the picture of profound grief. Thinking of his own girl,

Dee realized, wishing *he* had a body to place in a coffin, a marker to show his daughter had lived and died, a place he could visit and leave flowers. That's all people needed to make a death real, to see the coffin go into the ground and know where the body lay. France had large cemeteries of Canadian war dead, but that knowledge brought little comfort to families in Price's Corners and Wallen that had sons buried on foreign ground.

Mary Ann's parents stood nearest the coffin, Mrs. Simpson clutching her husband's arm. Her coat hung loosely on her frame, the flesh eaten from her body by four years of torment and uncertainty. Since Mary Ann's disappearance she'd not been able to work in the store, leaving her husband to run it by himself. Constable Carter, in his high-collared uniform, crisply pressed with buttons shining, and Mrs. Carter stood the closest to the Simpsons, as befitted their position in the village.

It was then that Dee realized there was a ring of empty space around her and Gran. Obviously, Dee thought bitterly, they were pariahs to be avoided as much as the gravediggers, who leaned on their shovels at the far end of the cemetery, patiently waiting to finish their work once the coffin was in the hole they had earlier dug. She reached for her grandmother's hand, something she hadn't done since she was a small child. Gran's gloved fingers entwined with Dee's own, and Dee felt comforted.

Reverend McAllister's voice droned on. Dee suspected he was enjoying the occasion and the large crowd and was drawing out the burial. From the corner of her eye, Dee saw movement among the gravestones. She glanced over and saw Clarence standing there, hat in hand, hair so golden it glowed like a small sun. Her heart beat quickly at the sight of him.

A final prayer, and the funeral was over. A lone red leaf drifted down from a nearby tree and landed on the raw earth. It lay there like a single drop of blood. Mary Ann was laid to rest.

People began to move toward the schoolhouse for the funeral lunch, knowing that when they came back out, the coffin would have been lowered, and dirt shovelled over it. Mrs. Carter touched a white handkerchief to her eyes and glared at Gran and Dee. She put an arm around Mrs. Simpson's shoulders. With a last look at the plain wood coffin, Mrs. Simpson meekly allowed herself to be led away.

Dee's grandmother stopped before Mr. Forgetti. She had noticed, as had Dee, the suspicious glances being thrown at him as people passed. Surely they didn't think he was a murderer? Dee thought. But then, to Price's Corners he was still a stranger, and better a stranger as a murderer than a friend or neighbour.

"I come to let the parents know that I feel bad for them. Mr. Simpson is always very kind to me," Mr. Forgetti said.

"It's a terrible thing," Gran said.

"I could not imagine losing one of my children. Not like this," he went on.

"How is Maggie?"

A smile lit up Mr. Forgetti's face. "She and the baby, they are doing fine. We thank you so much."

"That's good to hear," Dee's grandmother said. "Are you coming for the funeral lunch?"

Mr. Forgetti shook his head.

"It's a long way home for you. Have a bite to eat before you leave," Gran urged him.

After a moment, Mr. Forgetti nodded. "Thank you." He followed them across the yard and up the three steps into the schoolhouse. Because of the funeral, school had been suspended for the day. The schoolhouse was the largest building in the village and thus suited to hold a lunch of this size. On tables along one wall, breads and rolls, cold pork, cakes, and pies were laid out. The women of the village had all contributed food, Gran included. The stove had kettles set on it, and the fire was stoked high, much higher than Miss Hamilton would ever have allowed during school, but the water needed to boil so that the women could make coffee and tea.

Children ran about, chasing each other through the room. Occasionally, a mother would grab an arm as it passed and, for a few moments, her child was subdued.

Cissy came up to Dee and her grandmother, the baby in her arms and the toddler trailing behind holding onto her skirt.

Ray Price was with her, looking uncomfortable in a shabby suit jacket.

"I will need you in a few months," Cissy said softly.

Gran shook her head. "No. You need the doctor this time." She looked over to Cissy's husband. "You nearly died during the last birth. I told you there should be no more children. You need the doctor to see to this one if you're going to live." Dee's grandmother raised her voice slightly and looked directly at Ray Price. "And you need more rest right now, too, Cissy."

Ray Price ducked his head. "I got work waiting for me," he said and left. He didn't take kindly to Gran telling him what to do.

"I'll come over after school and help you with the house-work," Dee offered.

Clooey came up and touched Dee's arm. "The older girls are going to serve the food," she said.

Dee turned to her grandmother for permission to leave, but Gran was staring across the schoolhouse, her attention focused on Vivien, who glided across the room with a pot of tea. She'd cleaned herself up for the funeral, hair tidy beneath a blue bow. She really was beautiful, Dee thought.

"Gran?"

Eyes still locked on Vivien, her grandmother nodded for Dee to go, but before she could move, Mrs. Carter blocked her way.

"I cannot believe you have the gall to show your face here,

Mrs. Vale," she cried. "It's a travesty. You are only adding to Mrs. Simpson's grief."

"Maude," Constable Carter said sheepishly into the suddenly silent room.

His wife swept around to confront him. "You should be arresting her right now. You know she had a hand in that girl's death. And probably in those other girls' deaths, too."

Mrs. Carter turned back to Dee and her grandmother. "In another time, you would be burned at the stake."

"In another time," Dee's grandmother said, "you'd be put in stocks for your gossiping ways."

"Ladies." Chief O'Brien stepped between them. "Constable, control your wife."

A hand grasped Dee's shoulder. "Tell me who did this terrible thing to my girl. Tell me!" Mrs. Simpson fell to her knees, dragging Dee down with her. She winced as the woman's fingernails cut through her blouse and into her skin.

"Everyone says you have the sight. You were with her all the time. You must know who killed her. Who took my girl from me? You need to tell me!" Mrs. Simpson's voice rose with every word until the final one came out as a shriek.

"I don't know, Mrs. Simpson. I really don't." Scared, Dee looked about wildly for someone to rescue her. Clooey, she would help. . . . But the girl's mother held her daughter back. Finally, Dee locked eyes with Mrs. Hughes. The room receded and Dee felt herself drowning in the woman's terror and pain.

"Let go of the girl. She doesn't know who hurt Mary Ann." Dr. Hughes gently loosened Mrs. Simpson's grip from Dee's arm and raised the woman to her feet. He nodded to Mr. Simpson to take his wife. "I'll get her something for her nerves," the doctor said.

He reached down again and helped Dee up, then turned to Gran. "Perhaps it would be best if you and Dee left, Mrs. Vale. Your presence here appears to upset Mrs. Simpson."

A soft sigh and a thud and all eyes turned from Dee and her grandmother. Mrs. Hughes had fainted. In the resulting commotion, Dee's grandmother pushed Dee ahead of her out of the schoolhouse.

Mr. Forgetti followed. "I'll give you a ride home."

Dee stumbled down the steps of the schoolhouse, unable to see because her eyes had filled with tears.

Later, squashed between Mr. Forgetti and Gran on the wagon seat, she spoke. "How could they do that, Gran? Even Clooey didn't stand up for me, and we're best friends."

"It's not Clooey's fault or even her mother's," Gran replied.

"But you give them syrups and teas for Mister's lungs!"

"They're just scared. Those people are all looking at each and wondering who among them, who of everyone they've known their entire lives, committed this dreadful murder."

"But most people say it was a stranger, a tramp, or someone travelling through."

"Or me," Mr. Forgetti put in. "I see them looking at me. I hear them. People, they get scared and they start thinking all kinds of bad things."

The wagon bumped over a stone in the road, throwing Dee against Mr. Forgetti.

"That's just their way. Maggie and the rest of us, we know you're a good man," Gran said.

"Still, when people are scared, bad things happen," he went on.

"Do you really think it's one of them?" Dee asked fearfully. She wasn't any different from the rest of them, wanting so much for the murderer to be a peddler, or someone from the city. She couldn't imagine a single one of their neighbours as a killer.

"I don't know," Gran said. "I helped birth many of these people. I can't imagine a single one as a cold-blooded murderer.

"And don't mind Clooey," her grandmother continued. "Her mother has so much on her plate right now she doesn't know which way to turn, and it's confusing for Clooey."

Dee wiped her eyes on her sleeve. Gran was right. Clooey didn't complain much, but Dee saw how she had to take care of her brothers and sisters and help her mother more and more as her father got worse.

"That was odd," Mr. Forgetti said. "The doctor's wife; what make her faint?"

"I guess she's afraid like the rest of us, but with some people it just goes deeper. Mrs. Hughes is quite delicate," Gran answered.

"I think she's haunted," Dee said, remembering the woman's terrified gaze. "By a bad memory or . . ." Dee couldn't explain any further.

Mr. Forgetti stopped the wagon outside their house. "Remember what I said. People who are scared do bad things. They don't think clearly. You two alone . . ." He looked troubled.

"We'll be just fine," Gran said.

With a wave he drove away.

Dee's grandmother walked up the path toward the door, but Dee held back. "Gran, why were you looking at Vivien at the funeral lunch? You were staring at her."

Her grandmother looked over at the old Martin house. "I'm not sure," she said. "It's like there's a veil over that girl. I can't see through it. Probably nothing."

Dee doubted that it was nothing if it bothered her grandmother so much, but she just nodded. "I'm going up the mountain for a bit."

Her grandmother hesitated for so long that Dee thought she would be forbidden to go, but finally all Gran said was, "Be careful, and be back before dark."

CHAPTER TWELVE

It is safe as a church up here, Dee assured herself, but then jumped as a squirrel leapt noisily from one tree to another. Nervously looking from left to right, she stumbled on unearthed roots, regained her footing, and looked up to find herself facing a man. She screamed before she realized it was Podge. He flailed about, terrified himself.

"Podge, it's me. Dee!" she shouted as she ducked a flying fist.

"Oh. Oh," Podge said. Large hands dropped to his side. "Dee."

"I'm sorry I screamed. I didn't mean to scare you. I didn't expect you to be here. Why aren't you at the funeral lunch?"

"It's sad there," Podge said. "It's sad here, too," he continued.

"I know," Dee said. He was right: the trees, the air, the sullen sky seemed saturated with sorrow.

Podge shifted his feet and shot fearful glances around the woods. "She was sad," he said.

"Who?" Dee asked. The carved bird that was still under

her pillow came to the forefront of her mind. Why hadn't she thrown it into the fire yet?

"Mary Ann," Podge said. "She's sad to be dead."

Dee took a step back, suddenly aware of Podge's size, his large hands. But Podge, he wouldn't have hurt Mary Ann. He didn't have that in him, did he? No! Dee hated herself for thinking bad of Podge even for a minute. He had no evil in him. He must be referring to the sadness of the funeral.

"Why don't you go home?" Dee suggested. "Your mother will be wondering where you are."

Podge nodded. "I'll go home. Bye," he said, and lumbered down the path that Dee had just climbed up.

Dee watched him go until he was out of sight, then continued to climb. "Nervous Nellie," she chided herself. But it was with relief that she pushed through hanging grapevines and brush, leaving behind the shadowy trail for the daylight of her rock chair. She walked to the edge, took a deep breath, and felt the tension fade away. Being scared by misshapen trees, small creatures in the underbrush, and Podge seemed silly now that she was out in the open.

Fog obliterated all below her. She could hear the falls, the scream of a jay, and the melancholy sound of dripping water nearby. There really wasn't much here today to comfort her. She turned to go home and shrieked. Clarence stood behind her. Lost in her own thoughts, she hadn't heard his footsteps on the rock. Her heart pounded, but whether it was from fright or with joy, she didn't know.

"You scared me," Dee said to hide her fluster. "You shouldn't sneak up on people like that."

"I'm sorry." Chastened, he hung his head.

Dee immediately was sorry for her sharp words. "It's not your fault. It's everything that's going on today." Tears threatened to overflow. She blinked rapidly.

Clarence nodded. "I was at the cemetery."

"I saw you there. It was my friend, Mary Ann's funeral . . ." Dee couldn't say anything else.

"I heard talk that they only had her bones to bury," Clarence said gently.

Dee nodded. "She disappeared four years ago. I thought she'd run away to get married, but she was up here all that time. She and I used to have a secret place underneath a big spruce tree. That's where they found her."

"How did she die?" Clarence asked.

"Chief O'Brien said someone hit her over the head and stabbed her. She was murdered. But . . . I don't think she was killed under that tree. I think she was killed somewhere else and later brought there." Dee spoke slowly, trying to work it out in her own head.

"Why do you think she wasn't killed there?" Clarence asked.

Dee thought fast. She couldn't very well tell him that she could *feel* a person's death and that she didn't *feel* Mary Ann's beneath the tree. He'd think her a lunatic. "Because you wouldn't be able to dig a grave under that spruce. There are too many roots. I don't think a murderer would leave her exposed like that. He'd want to hide her body." She hoped that made sense.

"I think someone knew we played there," she continued, then stopped, horror-stricken. The idea that someone had watched her and Mary Ann go up the mountain, knew exactly where they went, terrified her. Was someone watching her right now? Dee darted a look around, but everything appeared normal. Still, she lowered her voice. "I think she was murdered and buried somewhere else originally and later moved under the tree."

"Murdered." Clarence's hands curled into fists. He stood, opening and shutting them as he stared into the mist. "No matter where you go, it seems there is always someone wanting to do harm to someone else. You shouldn't be up here by yourself," he said.

"I'm not scared," Dee protested, though she was now deathly afraid. "I'm not letting someone keep me away from my mountain. It's the only place I get to be alone. At home Gran is always after me to do chores: feed Trojan—that's our pig—take care of the chickens, weed the garden, grind up herbs, go to birthings with her. Between that and school I don't get a minute to myself. Besides, Mary Ann died four years ago. Whoever did it is probably long gone."

"So you think it was a stranger?"

Dee hesitated. She badly wanted to say yes. "I don't know," she said finally.

"Still, be careful," Clarence said. "It's been my experience that the worst villain can have the most benign face."

"My gran says it is hard to detect evil because it wears a good disguise." She thought of the black pillar and shuddered.

"Your grandmother sounds like a very wise woman, even if she does work you too hard," Clarence said. He grinned and Dee couldn't help but grin back. He had the nicest smile, she decided. And the nicest eyes.

"So?" Clarence raised his eyebrows. "Is this the day you show me the waterfall?"

"If you like." All thoughts of going home were gone now.

Dee went back through the underbrush and began to work her way carefully down a slight incline, ankle-deep in yellowed leaves. Clarence followed. Dee had once slipped on a pine cone, of all things, and found herself somersaulting down the side of the mountain until a sturdy tree trunk broke her fall. She didn't want to find herself with her skirt over her head with Clarence behind her.

A little while later, she stopped at the lip of a large, jagged gouge in the earth. Far below, between steep rock walls, a river frothed white. As she waited for Clarence to catch up, she felt warmth on her face and looked up to see watery sunshine melting the fog. She took off her coat and folded it over her arm. She'd have to be careful not to tear her good dress, worn for the funeral, but she was glad she had it on, knowing its deep green reflected her eyes. "You're vain," she scolded herself quietly, but couldn't stop a small bubble of happiness from forming.

The dull roar of the falls had grown to a thunderous booming. "We have to go down here," she shouted. "It's the easiest way to get to the falls. Watch the rocks. They get slippery from the spray."

Placing their feet into niches carved by weather into the stone wall, they descended into the gorge. At the bottom, they followed the riverbed around a bend and came to the falls. Water thundered over the cliff to hit a churning pool below with a deafening roar.

"They're called Brewsters' Falls," Dee said.

To her right a smaller waterfall, a mere trickle compared with the large one, meandered its way down the tiers of the rock wall, but it was the strength of the large one that never failed to excite Dee. Spray misted her face, and her ears rang. The ground beneath her feet trembled with the waterfall's force. A memory came to her of Mary Ann squealing with fright when Dee had first shown it to the girl. Instead of admiring the falls, Mary Ann had complained that she was getting wet and wanted to leave. Dee waited to see how Clarence would react.

"It's beautiful," he yelled over the roar.

"My friend Clooey and I usually sit over there, out of the spray." She pointed behind her to a slab of stone sheltered by three thin weather- and water-beaten trees. Clooey liked the falls as much as Dee, though it had been a while since she had visited them. Responsibilities at home had kept both of them away this past summer.

Dee sat on the ledge, feet swinging. Not very ladylike, she knew, but she didn't care. It felt good to be free of the village, free of the sudden silences and sidelong glances that greeted her now. Clarence lowered himself beside her and swung his legs, too. He took off his army cap and set it beside him. His hair gleamed in the sun.

"Why do you still wear your uniform?" Dee asked.

Clarence looked down at himself, as if he'd never considered his clothing before. He shrugged. "I guess because I have nothing else to wear."

Dee's cheeks burned red with embarrassment. She hadn't meant to shame him.

Clarence got up and walked over to a slight rise of dirt behind them. "What's this? There's a gravestone here."

"It's an old grave," Dee told him. She didn't tell him about the bitter-eyed young man who occasionally materialized next to it, his anger at having died so young keeping him tied to the falls.

She joined Clarence and read the epitaph carved into the stone. "*Come near my friends and cast an eye. Then go your way prepare to die. Learn here your doom, and know you must. One day like me be turned to dust.*"

"The story goes that he drowned after an argument with his parents. He'd stormed out and somehow ended up falling into the river. They buried him here because this is where he was found and it was his favourite spot."

"It must have been difficult to carry that heavy stone down here," Clarence said, looking up at the cliffs. "And then finding a place where the soil was deep enough to bury him. Still, it's a pretty place to spend eternity."

"Another girl drowned here, Mr. Richmond's daughter, Elizabeth, though they never found her body. I didn't know her because it happened before I was born. Podge found her coat downriver, and that's why they thought she'd drowned." *Podge. The carved bird.* She pushed the unwelcome thought out of her mind. "No—not Podge. Mr. Richmond is the man I was telling you about who owns the mill."

Dee stared at a boulder in the middle of the river, large enough to split the river into two channels. It was odd, though, she thought. If Mr. Richmond's daughter had drowned here, shouldn't she *feel* it? Surely, that cruel a death would have left some impression. But perhaps because the river flowed continuously, it didn't keep energy around.

"So two girls died up here?" Clarence said. He put his hat back on his head.

Dee sighed. She'd started this conversation, so she may as well finish it. "And a couple of other girls went missing on the mountain. But that was a long time ago, too."

"Still, that seems like a lot of deaths . . . and all were girls." Clarence's voice trailed off. He stared at the river.

But Dee didn't want to think about death right now, not with Clarence beside her and the sun now shining brightly from a blue, blue sky. She left the grave and went to sit on the ledge again. After a moment, Clarence sat beside her.

"This river runs all the way to Lake Ontario. That's miles away," Dee said. Geography should be a safe subject. "Though you saw the ocean when you went overseas, so this river won't seem all that interesting."

"It's a beautiful river. Crossing the ocean by ship made me very ill," Clarence said. "I was never so glad to see land as when we docked in England."

"I know you were at war, but it must have been a bit of an adventure to see all those different places," Dee said.

He picked up a stick and tossed it into the river. They watched it pick up speed and shoot through the foam and into quieter water.

"I admit that when we started out it was exciting. I'd never been out of the city very much, and here I was crossing the Atlantic Ocean. England wasn't too bad, except for the rain . . ."

He grimaced. "I'm surprised I didn't have mushrooms growing out of my ears. That and the fact we trained all the time—well, it got tedious after a while. But once we got to France, everything changed. The adventure part was over. It was a nightmare."

Clarence sat silent for a moment, his hands hanging between his knees, head bent. "Do you know who the wounded and the dying call for?"

Dee shook her head.

"Their mothers. We were just boys over there. Playing at being men, yet when we were hurt or dying, we wanted our mothers. And the real men, the grown ones, the officers who planned the battles? They sat safe in their tents or their offices, behind the lines, and ordered those boys over the top to be gunned down. Those men didn't see the death. They didn't hear the boys crying for their mothers, so they just kept sending us out. Maybe if they'd heard . . ."

"I'm so sorry," Dee said. She felt helpless in the face of such anguish.

"No," Clarence said. "I'm sorry. I shouldn't be talking like this to you."

Dee watched a spider scurry across the sun-warmed rock. "I've seen death before, though not from war. I don't mind you talking."

Clarence turned to her and smiled. Dee's heart somersaulted when she saw the dimple in his right cheek.

"I've never been farther than Wallen," Dee told. "My

mother left me right after I was born. She likes to sing, so she's with a travelling show, seeing the world. She sent me a seashell. That's the closest I've ever been to the ocean," she added shyly.

"You might still see it someday," Clarence told her.

"Maybe." She shrugged. "I hope to take up training to be a nurse. I'll have to leave Price's Corners to do that." There. She'd said it out loud. Now it seemed real, like something she might actually do.

"The nurses overseas were wonderful," Clarence said. "They took good care of us. I think you'd make a really fine nurse."

Dee grinned.

"What does 'Dee' stand for? Diane?" Clarence asked.

"No. It's for Defiance. My mama named me that."

"Defiance?" He laughed. "It suits you. I can see now why you aren't scared to be out here alone. So tell me, who was the skinny man with the stout, fussy-looking wife?"

"At the funeral?" Dee asked.

Clarence nodded. "In the police uniform. Though it *seemed* like the woman was wearing the pants, if you know what I mean."

"Oh, that would be Constable Carter, and I guess Mrs. Carter *is* fussy-looking, isn't she?" Dee giggled. "She's head of the Temperance Society against the Evils of Alcohol."

"She should be head of the Interfering and Fussy Women Society," Clarence suggested.

Dee laughed. She suddenly felt very happy sitting with Clarence, telling him all about Mrs. Carter's terrible cooking and Constable Carter's bullying, about Reverend McAllister relishing her name, Simpsons' store, and Cissy Price and her children. And for a little while, she forgot about murder and hoped—hoped—he had forgotten about the war.

CHAPTER THIRTEEN

G ran had gone to a birthing, and for the first time ever had left Dee behind.

"I'm missing too much school," Dee had protested. She had then gone on to tell Gran that if she was old enough to care for Trojan and the chickens, and that, as Gran often told her, some girls her age were already married, she was certainly old enough to stay one night alone. Faced with her own arguments, Gran had reluctantly agreed.

"Be in before dark. It's Hallowe'en," her grandmother said as the expectant husband hurried her away in the early hours of the morning. "Take care."

Gran didn't have to worry. Dee would be in the house with the door locked before night fell. From the time she was small, Gran had not allowed her to wear a mask or costume on Hallowe'en, saying, "You don't need to be something other than what you are." When she was older, and resentful of missing the Hallowe'en parties her friends went to, Gran explained further: "On Hallowe'en night, the boundary that separates the world of the living and dead thins, allowing the dead to return. Some want to cross over to see a loved one, and a few have less charitable purposes. But other creatures walk that night, too. Creatures that mean to do you harm. On Hallowe'en night you are vulnerable, as good and evil walk side by side."

Hearing that, Dee readily agreed to stay in while others went to parties. She would not go to the Young People's Society's Hallowe'en social at the schoolhouse that night, though there was to be a fortune teller. All the girls at school were excited, and Dee did admit to a certain curiosity, but she didn't need to *see* what was walking this night.

The day had dawned unseasonably warm, as a weak sun fought to punch holes in the high, wispy clouds. The wind blew steadily from the southeast, a soft blow, the kind that promised rain. Already this early in the morning, as Dee fed Trojan and the chickens, she was aware of restlessness in the air, anticipation. If everyone could feel it, would there even be a Hallowe'en, she wondered?

As she passed Vivien's house on the way to school, she looked around hopefully but didn't see Clarence. In fact, no one from the house was waiting to walk to school with her. She continued down the road to the Haynes's farm, where Billy pushed himself away from the tree trunk he had been leaning against. He fell into step with her.

"Where's Vivien?" asked Dee.

"She's gone off me," he said.

"That's too bad."

"I don't mind. She was a bit hard to talk to. Not like you. You always have something interesting to say." He grinned at Dee.

Inwardly she groaned. Was he thinking she was his girl-friend again? She'd better set him straight right away. She hurried her steps. "I want to speak to Miss Hamilton about extra studying. I want to be sure I'm prepared for the school in Wallen next year," she said, hoping Billy would get the message.

"I don't know why you like school so much," Billy complained. "I'll be glad to be out of it. If I'd had my way, I would have been done with it last year, but you know Ma.

"It's Hallowe'en today," Billy continued slyly.

"I know," Dee answered.

"Are you going to the party tonight?" he asked.

Dee shook her head. "No. And if you come to my house and play a prank on me, I'll never talk to you again, Billy Haynes."

He snorted back a laugh.

They came upon Podge, waiting at the side of the road for them, his face long with misery. "Esther didn't come today," he said.

"Maybe she's gone off you like Vivien's gone off me," Billy told him.

Dee threw an exasperated look at Billy. "She probably has to help her mother at home. I'll be your girlfriend for today."

Podge nodded, a little more cheerful now, and grabbed Dee's hand in his own. Dee was surprised all over again at how big Podge's hands were, how strong the fingers. Then Podge bent down to plant a kiss on Dee's lips. Dee pushed him back. "Don't do that!" she scolded him.

"But Esther says boyfriends kiss their girlfriends," Podge protested. He pursed his lips again.

"No." Dee freed her hand. "I'm just a pretend girlfriend, so you can't kiss me. And Esther is too young to be kissed. You stop doing that."

Darn Vivien and her family, changing everything. Podge had never wanted to kiss her before. She was beginning to wish they'd never moved here—but then she wouldn't have met Clarence.

"You can't kiss her anyway, because she's *my* girlfriend," Billy added. "I'm just lending her to you for the day."

"I am nobody's girlfriend," Dee said firmly.

They arrived at the school to find Clooey standing outside the gate, rather than by the swings as usual. As she got closer, Dee saw tears flooding Clooey's grey eyes.

"What's the matter? Is Mister worse?" Dee asked anxiously.

Clooey shook her head. "No. He's the same. But . . ." The tears spilled over, running down her cheeks. "I'm not going to school anymore, Dee," she said. "With Mister not able to work and Ma needing to take care of him, I have to start bringing in a wage. I'm going to be working in Wallen, as a maid for Mrs. Hughes. It was all arranged the afternoon of the funeral, though Ma didn't tell me until last night. I'll make seventy-five cents a day plus my room and board. I start tomorrow. I've already told Miss Hamilton. I was just waiting to tell you before I go home and pack."

Dee's chest constricted. "But I thought we would be going to school together next year in Wallen. I thought we were going to board together," Dee cried.

"There's no money for school," Clooey said. "There's not even enough money for food for the children. You're the smart one, anyway. You're the one who should go to high school. Not me. But I'll be home every other weekend," she added through her tears.

Dee hugged her friend. "I'll miss you dreadfully."

"I'll be at the Hallowe'en party tonight. Ma said I could go, since I leave tomorrow. Couldn't you come, just this once? Maybe the fortune teller will study my hand and say that I will marry a rich man. Maybe she will tell you that, too, and we will spend our afternoons together taking tea," Clooey finished grandly.

Dee shook her head. "I can't come to the party. Gran's away at a birthing and she made me promise I'd stay in after dark," she said. She forced a smile for Clooey's sake, though she felt her heart breaking. "You go and have a good time."

She had known the day would come when they all would split up and go separate ways. That was the way life was, but she hadn't thought it would come so soon.

"I've never been away from home before," Clooey said anxiously.

"The days will pass really fast, and I'll be at church week after next and see you there," Dee promised. She gave Clooey a final hug and stood at the fencing, watching the other girl walk away.

Dee spent the day at school lost in her thoughts, barely noticing the excitement of the children as they waited impatiently for dark and the party. The little ones had made masks and were running around the schoolyard at recess scaring each other. Dee watched them from where she sat on the bottom step of the schoolhouse, trying to sort out her feelings. Why did everything have to change? Maybe she should stay in Price's Corners, where she knew everyone. Maybe she *should* marry Billy and settle into a life here. It would be sensible and safe. But ever since she'd seen that advertisement in the newspaper for pupil nurses, she had known in her heart that was what she wanted to do. So should she follow her heart or follow her head? The end of the school day brought the promised rain, but it had not brought Dee any closer to a decision.

Gran had asked her to stop at the store after school for sugar and black tea. Picking her way around puddles, Dee crossed the muddy street to the Simpsons' store, every footstep filled with dread. She hadn't been to the Mercantile since Mary Ann's bones had been found. She went up the wooden steps, took a deep breath to prepare herself, and pushed open the door. At first glance, the store appeared empty. Relieved, Dee shut the door behind her. That's when she saw Mrs. Carter looking over a length of dark green serge at the back of the store. Dee considered leaving but knew Gran needed the supplies.

"Three dollars is a bit steep," Mrs. Carter complained to Mr. Simpson.

"It would be three dollars and fifty cents in the city, Mrs. Carter. It's a fine material. You won't find any better than that for a nice coat," Mr. Simpson assured her.

Dee tiptoed over to the long counter that ran along the side and winced when the wood floor creaked, announcing her presence. The tea and sugar were in large jars on shelves behind the cash register. She needed Mr. Simpson to weigh the goods out for her.

"I'll be right with you," Mr. Simpson called.

After a few minutes, he left Mrs. Carter to ponder the fabric and went behind the counter. "How are you keeping, Dee?" he asked kindly.

"Fine, Mr. Simpson," Dee said. "We need a pound of black tea and five pounds of brown sugar. How is Mrs. Simpson?" she asked politely.

He pulled the jar of tea from the shelf and set it on the counter. He laid a fresh piece of paper down and scooped tea leaves onto it, then put it on the scale. "Still poorly at times, but I have my hopes that she will soon be doing better. She's out most days, now, though it is just to the cemetery to visit . . ." He lost his words inside grief for a moment, cleared his throat, and went on. "Still, she's out and that's an improvement."

Dee nodded.

"She is prostrate with grief." Mrs. Carter came up to the counter. "And how else would she be with her daughter lying in the churchyard?"

Dee heard the store door open behind her, and shut. Another customer.

Mr. Simpson glanced over her shoulder and nodded a welcome to the newcomer. "Be right with you." He turned back to Dee. "And that was five pounds of brown sugar?"

"Yes," Dee whispered. She wished she could make herself invisible.

The newcomer had brought the scent of tobacco mixed with woodsmoke into the store, along with the pungent odour of soap and medicine and rubbing alcohol, and, underlying it all, the faint sour smell of illness. Dee didn't need to turn around to know it was Dr. Hughes.

"Mr. Simpson, I need you to cut me six yards of the green serge," Mrs. Carter demanded.

"As soon as I'm finished with Dee," the shop owner said. He scooped sugar onto a scale. "I won't be but a moment."

Mrs. Carter pursed her lips. "Good afternoon, Dr. Hughes," she said.

"Good day, Mrs. Carter. I stopped in to get my pipe tobacco. I've been in Price's Corners most of the day and ran out."

"Is someone ill?" Mrs. Carter asked avidly.

Looking for gossip, Dee knew.

"No, just the usual colds and ailments," Dr. Hughes replied.

"Mr. Simpson, you should not keep the busy doctor waiting, nor myself, for that matter, to serve this girl," Mrs. Carter said.

"I'm not in a hurry," Dr. Hughes said mildly.

That silenced Mrs. Carter for a few minutes. Dee mentally urged Mr. Simpson's fingers to work faster at tying her parcel, before Mrs. Carter could find her tongue again.

"Now, Dee, have you heard from your mother recently?" Mrs. Carter asked. She'd found it, and had whittled it into a sharp dart.

"Not recently," Dee replied shortly.

"You have to wonder at some people who just up and leave their children. I know if I'd been blessed with children I could never do that. But some people just don't seem to care what becomes of their children."

Mr. Simpson's hands stopped in mid-knot. His face paled.

Dee was horrified. Didn't the woman realize what she was saying in front of the grieving storekeeper?

"Mind you, if your mother had been married, matters might have been different."

Recovering, Mr. Simpson finished the knot and handed the package to Dee.

"Gran says she'll settle up with you next week," Dee said hurriedly. She wanted nothing more than to be out of the store.

"That's fine," Mr. Simpson assured her, then turned to Mrs. Carter. "Madame, it is true that I rely on the goodwill of the people of this town for my livelihood. But this is my store, and Dee is a welcome customer here and was a dear friend of my late daughter. I will not have you speak to her or me in such a fashion in my mercantile."

Dee didn't know who was shocked more, her or Mrs. Carter. The woman's mouth opened and closed like a fish gasping for air.

Mr. Simpson bent and fished out pipe tobacco from under the counter. Dr. Hughes rummaged in his pocket and brought out some bills and change, which he placed on the counter, then scooped up the tobacco. He put his hand on Dee's shoulder and steered her out of the store.

"Whenever I run into Mrs. Carter," he said as he and Dee went down the store steps, "I'm doubly sorry for Constable Carter."

Dee smiled.

"Would you like a ride home?" he asked.

Dee shook her head. "I'm going to Cissy Price's. It's not far." She wanted to walk and clear her head.

Dr. Hughes opened his car door. "Your friend Clooey is coming tomorrow to help out my wife. You're welcome to visit her any time you're in Wallen."

"Thank you," Dee said. She hesitated, and as he began to step into the car, asked, "Dr. Hughes, do you know anything about pupil nurses?"

He stepped back out, shut the door, and leaned against it, one foot propped up on the running board. "So, you want to be a nurse?"

Dee nodded. "I saw an advertisement in the newspaper for pupil nurses. It was from a Chicago hospital."

"You wouldn't have to go that far," he said. "You can go to a hospital in Toronto for training. It's not an easy task, though. Some girls have romantic ideas of being a nurse."

"I'm not afraid of hard work and I don't have any romantic ideas," Dee told him.

Dr. Hughes laughed. "No, I don't imagine you do. And you've seen a lot of illness from working with your grandmother. Mind you, it would mean leaving Price's Corners and living at the hospital while you trained. But they would be happy to get you. Nurses are in short supply." He studied her carefully. "I'm in a hurry right now. Perhaps next time we meet we can discuss this further."

"Thank you," Dee said.

The doctor smiled, got into his car, and drove away. Dee cradled her school books and the packages of tea and sugar against her chest and began to walk, her thoughts scattered everywhere. It had been an upsetting day.

Mrs. Carter was a thoroughly disagreeable woman, but she'd only said what Dee herself had thought many times. How could Mama just up and leave her? True, she'd left her with Gran, and Gran had taken good care of her, but didn't Mama ever wonder how Dee turned out? Didn't she want to see her daughter?

And what about her father? Dee often shied away from the fact that she had to have had a father. Of course, everybody did, but she didn't like thinking about it. But didn't he ever wonder about her? Was it someone from Price's Corners? Or Wallen? Dee thought over the men of the town but couldn't fit any of them to any part of her, so decided it had to have been someone from far away whom her mother had met and fallen in love with. Now that, she thought, was the kind of silly romantic thought she had just told Dr. Hughes she didn't have. But it did sometimes happen that way. Girls got caught out, because their hearts ruled rather than their heads.

She turned into Cissy's to make good on her promise to help with the housework. She arrived in the kitchen to find a weary-looking Cissy surrounded by hungry children, noisy and excited about the party that night. Dee shooed the boys

from the house and started the two older girls peeling potatoes.

"Sit down and put your feet up. I'll make you some tea,"
Dee ordered Cissy. While she waited for the kettle to boil,
Dee went outside to take in the laundry. As she folded a clean
sheet, she felt eyes upon her back. She whirled around to see
the familiar silver shimmer and, from behind it, a sad-faced
boy watching her. It's already started, she thought, and darkness not yet fallen.

"You go on now," she said gently.

The ghost boy looked longingly at the playing children.
He was about six or seven, dressed in overalls and a sweater.
A white bandage encircled his forehead. He'd obviously died
from a head injury, perhaps having fallen from a hay loft or a
moving wagon.

"There's nothing for you here amongst the living. You go
to your rest now."

With one last pleading glance at Dee, the boy faded away.
Dee's eyes filled with tears. Children were always the most
upsetting haunts to *see*. Taken before they had time to grow
up, most were bewildered and needed help to cross over. *Seeing*
this boy, though, left her nervous and aware that there were
more black streaks than blue in the sky as night approached.
She hurriedly fed Cissy's children an early supper and put a
plate of food in the oven to keep warm for Ray.

The older children left for the party, and without them

underfoot, Dee made short work of tidying the kitchen, but Cissy looked so tired that Dee stayed and put the younger children to bed, rocking the toddler until her eyes closed. Ray had still not come home.

"I guess he's working late at the mill," Cissy said with a sigh.

Dee nodded, but they both knew he was working at chasing down bootleg drink. He'd be hard to handle when he got home. Regardless, there was nothing Dee could do, so she pulled on her coat and gathered her books and packages.

"I'm off home now," Dee said.

"Are you all right in that house by yourself tonight?" Cissy asked.

"I'll be fine. If I get scared, I'll bring Trojan in to keep me company." She hoped she sounded braver than she felt.

Cissy laughed. "Off you go then, and thank you for all your help."

The temperature had dropped while Dee had been at Cissy's, and though the wind still blew hard, it had changed directions to come from the north, breaking up the clouds to reveal a large yellow moon. Bare branches danced wildly and dried leaves swirled around her ankles and crunched beneath her boots. That's the way it was with fall, Dee thought as she pulled her sweater tight across her chest. The day might be warm, but once the sun set, the temperature plummeted.

She stared at the wagon ruts stretching before her, glancing neither right nor left. Never before had she been out this late on Hallowe'en. The night crackled with energy, and from the corner of her eye, Dee could see the silver shimmers accompanying her home. So far she felt safe. None of these meant her harm. But she didn't know what lay ahead. She hurried, head down, eyes on the road, until she was startled by a silver haunt directly in front of her in the middle of the road. Dee's steps faltered, then stopped altogether. Mary Ann.

The dead girl took a step toward Dee, eyes begging, begging for help. Mary Ann's lips moved. "Dee." A whisper, like soft wind, rushed by Dee's ears.

But Dee didn't want to know what Mary Ann so badly wanted to tell her. She didn't want to hear who had killed the girl, didn't want to know.

"I can't help you," Dee said. "There's nothing I can do for you. You need to go and be with your baby."

Mary Ann drifted closer, her face taut, imploring Dee to listen, but Dee shook her head and made to step around the spirit. As she did, she heard the crunch of boots on dirt and stone behind her. Fearfully, she peered over her shoulder. A break in the clouds spilled white moonlight over the road, but there was no one to see. Just an animal, Dee told herself.

She turned her head back to find the road ahead of her empty. Thankfully, Mary Ann had left.

She quickened her pace, battling the wind, and once again

heard the footsteps, following her. She stopped and they stopped. A trick, Dee decided. A mean Hallowe'en trick.

She twirled around. "You just stop that, Billy Haynes!" she shouted. "You're not scaring me."

Arms full, she ran awkwardly past Vivien's darkened house. The steps pounded behind her, fast catching up. No spirit this, but a living thing, Dee realized. That's what Mary Ann had been trying to tell her! The girl's spirit had been trying to warn her!

Dee's breath came raggedly. She'd never make her house before being caught. Better to face whomever, or whatever, it was!

Dee stopped and whipped around again. This time she saw a man of medium height standing on the road, but she could not make out the face; it remained a hollow darkness. Wind wailed through the tops of the trees. If only she could *see* him, but he wasn't a spirit. This man was very much alive. He moved quickly toward her, a black blur. No human could move that fast, Dee realized with horror. She willed her feet to move, but they were rooted to the road.

"Run!" came Mary Ann's voice.

Suddenly, Dee's feet were free and in flight. She hazarded one backwards glance, only to see a whirlwind of leaves and dirt, Mary Ann in the centre, blocking the road, giving her a precious few seconds to escape.

Dee ran through her gate, threw open the front door,

slammed it closed behind her, and threw the bolt. Looking frantically around the room, she pushed the kitchen table against the door to block it. A skittering sound across the roof brought her head up. The *thing* was searching; searching for a way in! She banged shut the damper on the stove, heard the scratch of nails or claws on glass, and yanked the curtains across the windows. She ran into Gran's and then her own bedroom and made sure the windows were locked. Breathing hard, she stood, listening. All was quiet. Had it gone? A slam from the back of the house made her jump: the outhouse door. Just the wind, she tried to reassure herself. If you didn't latch it just right, the wind caught it. But she knew it wasn't the wind. Then she remembered the back door in the summer kitchen. It was always left open! Could she reach it before that—that thing did?

Sobbing, she grabbed a log from beside the stove and ran into the backroom. In the darkness, she tripped on a stool and went flying across the small room, falling in a heap beside the worktable. The latch rattled. Screaming, Dee picked herself up and then threw herself with all her weight against the door. It pushed back, but she managed to lock it. She stood guarding the door, the log raised above her head with two hands, ready to strike. All was quiet—until a loud banging on the stovepipe sent her running into the main room. A soft sigh at the window, then silence.

After a long while, arms shaking and legs no longer able

to hold her upright, Dee sank into her grandmother's rocking chair. She faced the door, wood ready at hand. She did not move for the rest of the night.

CHAPTER FOURTEEN

A pounding on the door jerked Dee out of an uneasy sleep. Disoriented, she wondered why she was in Gran's rocking chair, fully dressed, with a piece of firewood in her lap. Early morning light filtered through the curtains drawn over the kitchen window. Slowly it came back to her: Hallowe'en, the figure on the road, Mary Ann's spirit, running to the house and blocking the door with the kitchen table. A fist hammered against the door again.

"Who is it?" Dee yelled.

"Ray Price," a muffled voice replied.

Grunting with the effort, Dee pushed the heavy table back and opened the door a crack, still holding the log in her hand. Cissy's husband stood on the top step, scowling.

"Cissy made me come see if you were all right," he said.

Over his shoulder she saw a wagonload of men pass the gate, heading toward the mountain. A motor vehicle pulled up. Chief O'Brien and Constable Carter climbed out.

"Why? What's wrong?" she asked, alarmed by all the activity.

"Girl went missing. Never came home from the Hallowe'en party at the school last night."

"Who?" Dee's heart thudded painfully.

"That girl Clooey. I've got to go. Mr. Richmond closed the mill so we could all help search for her."

Dee grabbed the doorframe for support. Clooey! Maybe he was wrong. Maybe it was another girl. Clooey was going to the fortune teller at the party. She was going to be told that she'd marry a rich man. *The fortune teller!*

Dee ran out her gate to where Chief O'Brien, in his greatcoat, organized the men into search parties. She grabbed his sleeve. "Who was the fortune teller?"

"What?" Chief O'Brien asked distractedly.

Dee pulled her sweater closed. The weather had become very cold overnight. A light drizzle, mixed with snow, soaked the men's caps and jackets.

"At the Hallowe'en party last night. Who was the fortune teller? Maybe she knows where Clooey is."

"Leave the chief alone." Constable Carter pulled her away. "He's very busy."

"Clooey was going to the fortune teller," Dee babbled.

"I don't have time for your witchery. We have a girl to find," Constable Carter said. He gave her a small push toward the house. "You need to stay in and lock your door."

"It was teacher." Face pale, Billy Haynes stood with his father in a small knot of men. "Miss Hamilton put a kerchief around her head and had a glass ball. She was the fortune teller. Clooey was really disappointed, so she left the party early."

"You were there?" Dee asked. "You saw her?"

"Yes."

"Does everyone have their instructions and know where they're going?" Chief O'Brien shouted.

The men nodded.

"Then on your way."

"Wait," Dee said. "There was someone out last night. I was followed home from Cissy Price's house."

But Billy and the men didn't hear her as they set off to scour the mountain for Clooey.

"I saw someone on the road, too, last night." Vivien came up to Dee. "I was on our porch with the children, getting ready to leave for the party, and saw you running past. He was right behind you."

"Did you see who it was?" Dee asked eagerly.

Vivien shook her head. "At first I thought it was a person, but then it seemed to change shape and I thought it might be a big dog. It went around the side of your house. We left right after for the party, but we didn't see anything on the way to the schoolhouse.

"Don't *you* know who it is?" Vivien asked. "People say you and your grandmother can see things other people can't. They should have had you as the fortune teller, not Miss Hamilton. Then you could have told me my future. You could have told me if I was going to get out of here," Vivien said bitterly.

Surprised by the girl's vehemence, Dee looked closely at Vivien and saw the unhappiness in the girl's eyes. Vivien was miserable and small wonder, being stuck in that rundown house with an ill mother, and brothers and sisters to care for.

Dee wished with all her heart that Gran was there, but she was still at the birthing. She looked at the piece of firewood in her hand and knew what she had to do. "I have to go," she told Vivien and ran into the house.

She knew the mountain as well, if not better, than any of those men. She dropped the log and grabbed her coat. After buttoning it up, she tied a shawl over her head for extra warmth. She would find Clooey.

In the short time it took Dee to get ready, the drizzle had changed entirely to fat, wet flakes of snow that disappeared as soon as they touched the ground. To avoid the bridge and main path up the mountain, Dee crept around the back of the house and through the wintering kitchen garden to the stream. There it was an easy matter to jump from stone to stone to cross the shallow water. In the distance she could hear the men calling Clooey's name. She kept off the paths, knowing if the men saw her they would immediately send her home.

It was easier to push through the trees now that the

branches were bare and the undergrowth brown and wilted. As she climbed, the snow swirled more thickly, clinging to her eyelids and whitening her coat sleeves. Clooey would be cold. She was dressed for a party, not for snow. Never once did Dee let herself think that her friend might no longer feel the cold.

Blinded by the snow, Dee didn't see a protruding root that caught her toe and sent her tumbling head over heels down into a gully. She scrambled to her feet, wiped off the dirt and leaves from her skirt, examined a cut on her hand, then looked up to see Clarence in front of her. She let out a small shriek.

"Are you hurt?" Clarence asked.

"Just a scrape." Dee started to cry.

"What's going on? Why are there so many people out here?" Clarence asked.

"My friend Clooey," Dee sobbed. "She's missing. She went to the Hallowe'en party at the schoolhouse . . ."

Clarence nodded. "I was there for a while."

"She never got home," Dee continued. "Have you seen her? She has straight black hair and grey eyes."

"I remember her at the party. She was in a pretty blue dress with a feather mask on her face," he said. "She looked sad. But why would she come up the mountain, especially at night?"

"She wouldn't have. Not on her own. I think they're searching here because it's where they found Mary Ann's bones. And Clarence, I think she's up here, too. I think someone brought her here, or told her to come up the mountain. Maybe she was tricked. I'm so scared." Dee sobbed anew.

"I'll help the men with the search. You go back home where it's safe." Clarence turned to leave.

"No," Dee said. "I know this mountain as well as any of them. And if you stayed with me, I'd be safe then, wouldn't I?"

Clarence studied her a long time. "You'll just stay anyway, Defiance," he said wryly. "So I guess it's best if I'm with you." He sat down on a rock and pushed his hat back. "We need to think this out," he said. "Not just go stumbling all over the place. We need a plan." He stopped, then after a moment continued. "Where was that other girl found? The bones?"

"Mary Ann? Beneath a spruce tree where we used to play. I told you that, remember?"

Clarence looked momentarily confused, and then his face cleared. "Yes, but you didn't think she was killed there."

"Clooey's not been killed," Dee said. "I won't believe that. She's just—she's lost." Dee knew she sounded unconvinced herself. "She's probably hurt. Maybe she sprained her ankle. I did that once up here."

Clarence looked at her. "Yes, of course, you're right. She's hurt or lost. Would she look for shelter? I mean, she couldn't have walked too far at night. It would be hard to find your way in the dark."

"We all played in a field above here when we were kids. It's an open area with trees all around it." Including the spruce tree, but Dee didn't say that out loud. "Clooey would recognize it. She'd stay there if she was lost. She'd know I'd find her there."

"Lead the way, then," Clarence said.

Twenty minutes later, Dee and Clarence burst into an open field. They stood a moment looking out over beaten-down grass. Snow gathered in the dips and whitened the branches of the surrounding trees. The only sign of life was a bright red cardinal sitting on a brown stalk.

"Clooey!" Dee shouted. "Clooey!"

She waited, listening, but heard nothing except the strident scream of a blue jay and the steady knock of a woodpecker. Geese honked overhead, though Dee couldn't see them in the swirling snow. From far away, she could hear the men calling Clooey's name.

Clarence had walked out a little way into the field and was brushing the snow on the ground aside with his foot. "Dee, we need to search for any sign of the ground being disturbed."

"You mean like a grave," Dee said flatly.

"Or footsteps. Anything to show she's been here. I'm going to the far end over there." Clarence pointed to a line of trees. "You start searching here, and we'll meet in the middle."

Dee watched him cross the small field, then bent to the

task of carefully pushing aside dead leaves and snow with her feet. For an hour she kept her eyes glued to the ground, desperately wanting to find some sign of Clooey, yet at the same time terrified that she would. After a long while, she met Clarence in the centre of the field.

"She's not here," she said. Tears of frustration filled her eyes. Where could Clooey be? The mountain was such a large area for her to be lost in, they might never find her.

She took a step toward Clarence, stumbled, and cried out, clutching her head in pain.

"What is it?" Clarence asked, startled.

"Here! There's something here!" Dee bent down and parted the grass to reveal a long, narrow swelling in the ground. She pushed aside leaves and twigs that had been spread over it. The stain of black soil against the white snow confirmed that the hole was freshly made. "No! Oh, no!" Dee cried.

She frantically scooped earth from the mound with her hands until her fingers touched a swatch of light-blue cloth. She fell back, crawling quickly on all fours away from the shallow grave, distancing herself from the horror she knew lay there. Her head pounded. "That's Clooey's good dress, her blue dress." Her voice trembled.

"Call the men. I can hear them nearby," Clarence ordered. "I'm going to look around and see if I can find anything else."

Dee stood and shouted, "Over here! Over here!" then

crouched near the grave, covered her eyes with her shawl, and wept.

A few minutes later, hands helped raise her to her feet. Dee uncovered her eyes to see Chief O'Brien, Ray Price, and Dr. Hughes standing beside her, faces sombre at the sight of the heaped earth and the patch of blue cloth.

"I was afraid of this," Dr. Hughes said.

"I'll take Dee home." An arm went around her shoulder. "Dee, it's me, Billy."

"Where's Clarence?" Dee looked around the clearing.

"Who?"

Dee shook her head. It didn't matter. Nothing mattered anymore.

She shrugged Billy's hand off her shoulder. "I'm not going until I know for sure if it's Clooey buried there."

"Dee! Come away," Billy pleaded.

"No. I need to know if she's really dead."

More men arrived, some equipped with shovels. Dee gazed at the stricken faces of her neighbours. Constable Carter, Mr. Richmond, Mr. Forgetti, and even Mr. Simpson among them. She'd known these men all her life. Not one of them, she believed, could be capable of such a dreadful act. Yet, in front of her was a shallow grave. Someone in Price's Corners was a murderer.

"Put those shovels down for now," Chief O'Brien ordered. He gently brushed dirt from one end of the grave and pulled out a mask. He handed it to Dr. Hughes and bent again, clearing dirt until a nose, then a face appeared.

All of a sudden, Dee screamed and grabbed her head. Stabbing pain. Then her throat closed. No breath. As her knees buckled, she saw Billy's face swimming above her, then nothing.

Chapter Fifteen

Dee woke gasping, clawing at her throat, her eyes, her nose. Dirt filled them. He had thought she was dead and he'd buried her. But she was still alive. She moved her hand, plunged it through earth toward sky, and surprised him.

"You're home." A hand on her forehead, soothing. "You're safe in your bed." Gran.

Dee tried to focus on her grandmother's voice, but a shovel came through the dirt, hit her head, blinding pain, and she was sinking. So heavy, dirt piled on her body, face. She couldn't move. Then—nothing.

"Defiance. It is not your death. Let it go," Gran demanded.

There was no ignoring Gran now. Not when her grandmother had used Dee's full name for the first time that Dee could remember. She opened her eyes. Not the mountain, not a grave, but her own room, her own bed. She held her hands in front of her, saw the dirt black beneath her fingernails, and the horror all came back to her. Clooey was dead.

"There. She's coming to now." Dr. Hughes put his hand on

Dee's shoulder. "Just take it easy there, young woman. You'll be a little dizzy for a while."

Gran hovered above her, face pale and anxious. She held a cup to Dee's lips.

"Just a bit," she said.

Dee wanted to gulp the liquid to rid her mouth of the taste of earth, despite knowing she'd never had dirt on her tongue.

"I came as soon as I could. I knew you needed me, but it was a difficult birth. I couldn't leave." Her grandmother sounded distraught.

"Clooey's dead, Gran," Dee whispered.

"I know. I am so sorry." Gran pushed back a strand of hair from Dee's forehead. "I am so sorry."

"I felt her die." She closed her eyes. So tired.

"Is she awake? Can I speak to her?" Dee opened her eyes again to see Chief O'Brien looming over her, hat in hand, looking haggard.

Gran frowned, but stepped aside, though she didn't leave Dee's bedroom.

Over his shoulder, through the open bedroom door, Dee could see Billy, Cissy, and Constable Carter, and from the sounds of it, a lot of other folks were filling her and Gran's small house. And—Dee's heart began to pound—the other was here, too, in the house, the evil. She looked around fearfully for the black pillar. She couldn't see it, but that didn't matter. It was here. She could *feel* it!

"What time is it?" she demanded. She tried to see around the chief to the window, but Dr. Hughes blocked her view.

"It's just gone seven," Constable Carter said. He tried to crowd into the room, but Dee's grandmother pushed him out and shut the bedroom door.

"You've been sleeping most of the day, Dee. Billy brought you back around noon. Mrs. Price put you to bed and your grandmother arrived shortly after," Chief O'Brien said gently. "I'm sorry to have to ask you questions now, and I don't care about the hows or the whys of you knowing what you do. I just want to catch this monster. Can you tell me anything about how Clooey died?"

Clooey. She'd never see her friend again. Tears trickled from the corners of Dee's eyes.

"It's too much for her," Gran protested. "Let her rest."

"I wouldn't bother her if it wasn't important," Chief O'Brien insisted.

"He thought she was dead," Dee whispered. She put her hands to her chest, then her head. Pain. "He stabbed her in the chest, and he thought she was dead, but she wasn't.

"Dirt filled her nose, her mouth, her ears, her eyes. She couldn't breathe. Clooey tried so hard, but she couldn't breathe."

Heartrending sobs came from the other side of the door. "Why is Clooey's mother here?" Dee asked, upset by the sound of grief. "Why are all these people here?"

"She—they were hoping you could tell us what happened to Clooey," Gran explained.

After a moment, Dee went on.

"Her hand came up." Dee raised her own hand, fingers spread wide. "Up out of the dirt. It scared him. He thought she'd risen from the dead so he hit her head with the shovel. He sliced down through the dirt to her head, and he buried her again."

"Who was it?" Chief O'Brien asked.

Dee shivered. She was cold, yet so hot. Now she could see it, the dark pillar, churning near the door, stretching up to the ceiling. She turned her head away from it, terrified she'd see Clooey's screaming face alongside the others.

"I don't know. I can't see his face. Gran!" Dee cried. "Gran! Clooey is dead."

For a week, Gran kept Dee inside the house and cosseted her. Dee didn't mind. She couldn't get warm no matter how close she sat to the stove or how many quilts Gran piled on top of her, and the taste of earth lingered on her tongue. She was tired all the time and would have stayed in bed if her grandmother hadn't made her get up. She dreaded seeing anyone and didn't want to talk, though Chief O'Brien came back every day with the same question: Who? But she didn't have the answer.

"We're going to bring in a provincial detective from Toronto," Chief O'Brien told Dee and her grandmother in the late afternoon of the seventh day since Clooey died. He sat at their table, unshaven and tired, with new lines on his face. Dee doubted he had slept since Clooey's body had been found.

"They can handle this better than me. They know more about killers of this sort."

"This sort?" Dee asked.

"There's a type of person who kills for no known reason, and they don't stop killing until they are stopped," Chief O'Brien explained. "Most people kill because they want something: a new wife or a new husband, money, land. Greed causes a lot of deaths. But there are also those who are drawn to kill just for the sake of killing, and no one knows why. Sorry." He passed a hand over his face. "I shouldn't tell you this. I'm just so tired."

He soon left, but immediately there was a knock on the door. Gran went to open it, an axe in one hand, hidden within the folds of her skirt. She'd opened that door the same way for the past seven days, with that axe in hand. This time it was Billy and Vivien. They also had come to see Dee every day, Vivien surprising Dee with her concern. She hadn't thought the girl had caring in her. Gran left the three of them together, taking advantage of their keeping Dee company to feed the pigs and chickens. She wouldn't leave Dee on her own even for the short time needed to do the chores.

"Remember, don't let anyone in while I'm gone," she told Billy. "And call if you need me."

Dee had never seen her grandmother look so worn or so worried. She felt immensely guilty but couldn't rouse herself to do anything to help.

"Is school back in?" Dee asked. She felt she should be a bit social. After all, Billy and Vivien had taken the time to visit.

"Next week," Billy said. "After Clooey's funeral. Miss Hamilton says we all need a mourning period. She's gone home to Toronto." He shifted awkwardly on his chair, not liking to talk about the death of their friend.

"Dr. Hughes did the autopsy here, but he sent Clooey's stomach and heart and other parts of her to Toronto. Dr. Hughes said the laboratory at the university there can tell if she's been poisoned. Imagine that. They can tell how you died from your insides," Vivien said.

Dee shuddered and pulled a blanket tighter around her shoulders.

"You didn't need to tell her that," Billy protested.

"Oh, yes. I'm sorry, Dee," Vivien said.

Dee noticed that the girl's hair shone golden, freshly washed and neatly brushed, and her skirt had been lengthened with a ruffle added to the bottom. She actually looked happy, which annoyed Dee, but she reminded herself that Vivien hadn't known Clooey very long, so she wouldn't be too saddened by the girl's death.

"How are Clooey's mother and Mister?" Dee asked.

"Mister's not good. Dr. Hughes has been over to see him every day. Ma says it won't be long before he joins Clooey," Billy told her.

Dee's head sank onto her chest.

"It's horrible out there, Dee," Billy blurted out. He leaned forward. "Everyone's scared. People don't even talk out loud anymore, they whisper. And they look over their shoulders everywhere they go. The village is empty after dark. There weren't very many people at church on Sunday. Ma said you'd think they'd crowd the pews looking for comfort, but they're too frightened to even go to church."

"I'm sorry," Dee said, though she wasn't sure why she was apologizing. She hadn't done those awful things, but she still felt that she was somehow at fault, perhaps for not being able to tell Chief O'Brien who the killer was. But then, for the first time since Clooey's death, she felt the stirring of something inside. Surprised, she struggled to identify the emotion. Anger, she decided. She was very angry.

"How did you know?" Vivien asked.

"Know?" Dee echoed. She was still concentrating on the anger, feeling it spread to her fingers, tingling, then rush to her mind, banishing the inertia that had taken over her body the past week.

"How did you know where to find Clooey's body?"

"We used to play in that clearing, all us kids. So we thought maybe that was where she'd gone and she was there . . ." Dee faltered. Hadn't Clarence told Vivien about finding Clooey? And why hadn't he come around to see how she was doing? Well, she wasn't going to shame herself by asking Vivien about him.

"My dad and I had already gone over that entire clearing earlier and we didn't find a thing," Billy said.

"It was easy to miss. There were leaves covering it, and it was snowing hard. I almost fell over it, that's how I found it."

Billy got up and began to pace around the kitchen, hands in his pockets. "So you somehow *guessed* she was in that field and then somehow *found* the exact place."

"Yes," Dee said simply.

"You *guessed*," Billy said. "That's what I'm wondering. That's what everyone's wondering. How did you *guess* the exact spot?"

"I told you, I tripped on the piled-up dirt!" Dee said heatedly. "What do you want me to say? That I'm a witch? That I knew she was there? Very well, I am a witch." She threw the shawl off her shoulders, stood up, and faced him. It felt good to let the anger out, to feel the heat of it rage through her body, bringing her to life. "I *knew* Clooey was at that spot because I could *feel* what she felt."

She heard Vivien gasp but ignored the girl.

"I could *feel* her fear, her horror. I could *feel* the dirt being thrown on top of her, the blow to her head. It terrifies me that

I can *feel* that, but that's what happens to me. And I can *see* things, too. People who have died but not yet passed on. People held here by their own fear and bitterness and sadness and anger."

Billy took a step back from her.

Dee laughed harshly. "See? That is why I never tell anyone. You're afraid of me. I didn't ask to be this way, I just am."

"Can you see Clooey now?" Vivien looked around the room. She didn't seem all that bothered that Dee could see ghosts. "Is she here? Can she tell you who killed her?"

"No," Dee said. She fell wearily into her chair. The anger had passed, leaving her limp. "She's too new to death. And it was a violent death, unexpected. She doesn't know she's gone yet. It sometimes takes spirits a while to accept that they're dead and then learn how to show themselves."

Billy sat down in the chair opposite Dee but didn't take his eyes off her.

"Stop staring. I don't have an extra head," Dee said. "What I do, it's just something passed down in my family, like you have your dad's black hair."

"It's not quite like having black hair," Billy pointed out.

"No. It's not," Dee admitted. "It scares people. It scares you. Constable Carter thinks I can put a curse on him. But I can't. Besides, if I could, I'd put it on Mrs. Carter, not him."

Billy smiled briefly, while Vivien giggled.

"It's one of the reasons that I want to go away to where no one knows me."

"It doesn't matter where you go. You are what you are." Gran stood in the doorway. "You can't run away from yourself."

CHAPTER SIXTEEN

Unlike the misty gloom of Mary Ann's funeral, Clooey was laid to her rest under a blue sky, lightened by a bright sun, though its yellow rays carried no warmth. Dee had gone to the church service and shivered at the graveside in the cemetery but had slipped away up the mountain rather than go to the funeral lunch. It was cowardly to let Gran go to the schoolhouse alone, but Dee didn't think she could face people and their tongues; not with everyone talking about her.

There had been talk, too, from some of the men of going around the mountain and bringing in Mr. Forgetti. Chief O'Brien had put an end to those plans by saying that he'd throw in jail any man who bothered the Forgettis.

Other than her wandering about her own yard, it was the first day Dee had been out since Clooey's death. Her feet felt weighted down as she climbed up the mountain path, and she stopped to rest frequently. She'd lost all her strength since finding Clooey's grave. Sitting on a fallen tree trunk to catch her breath, she realized that her trip up the mountain was foolhardy. She'd told no one, not even Gran, where she was going. It had been instinct that led her feet here, because only on the mountain did Dee feel she could begin to make sense of all that had happened.

But how, she wondered, as she set off again, do you make sense of an irrational act, a murder? Finally, she made it to her ledge.

The fields and village spread below her, smeared into a messy canvas of shades of brown by her tears. She closed her eyes and saw Clooey's mother at the burial, numb with grief, and heard Mister's harsh cough mingled with the muffled sobs of Clooey's brothers and sisters, and dominating it all, she felt the suffocating fear that blanketed the village and all its people.

Looking at her neighbours around the gravesite, Dee had thought their shoulders more stooped, their faces more grim, the fear physically taking a toll on them.

The funeral was larger than Mary Ann's, people who didn't even know Clooey coming from miles around. Perhaps, Dee thought, they hoped that they would find some way to make sense of a senseless act. Many had also come to sympathize with Clooey's family. No one wanted to lose a child.

Also crowding the cemetery were reporters, even a few who had come all the way from the United States to the small village of Price's Corners to write about the funeral for their newspapers. The murder was big news in the United States,

Dr. Hughes told Dee's grandmother. Their small village was famous, he told them, but for the wrong reasons. Dr. Hughes stood alone at the funeral, his wife too ill to attend, as he told any who asked about her.

Too frightened to come, Dee believed, remembering the woman's terrified eyes. But why? Mrs. Hughes lived in Wallen and had a husband to protect her.

Standing on the ledge, thinking about Clooey, she felt Clarence behind her. He came to stand beside her, looking at the peaceful view below. "I'm very sorry about your friend."

"What kind of person would hurt someone as sweet as Clooey?" Dee asked tearfully.

"A monster," Clarence answered promptly. "There's nothing human about him."

"The worst thing is that it has to be someone from the village; someone from around here." Dee gestured toward the valley. "Someone I know, except I don't really know them, do I? Because I can't imagine anyone I know doing these horrible things. Why can't I *see* who killed Clooey?"

"Because he's evil," Clarence said. He was quiet for a moment. "It seems to me that there are two forces at work in this world. Good and evil. Like a tug-of-war at a picnic, if you take my meaning."

Dee nodded to show that she did.

"Sometimes evil gets ahead, but good always comes back and beats it down, you have to believe that," he continued. "But it's a constant battle to keep the upper hand. The war we fought in Europe was an example of that, though a large battle, but there are countless smaller ones going on all the time. Even sometimes *within* the larger fights. I am a witness to that. I am a witness to real evil. During the war, there was a man . . . an officer . . ." He stopped, shook his head, and went on. "I guess he figured, what are one or two more bodies when so many are dead? But it seemed so horrible that it was *him*. He'd be the last one I'd think to do such an unspeakable act. But I saw it with my own eyes." He stopped, uncertainty creeping into his voice. "And today, at the churchyard, I thought . . ."

"Thought what?" Dee prompted.

"Well, I was at the cemetery for the burying. And I thought I saw him. The man I saw in France, the man who enjoyed killing. But, it couldn't be. The chances that it was him are small. I mean, he could be anywhere.

"Probably just my mind playing tricks. It does that some-times, ever since the war." He paused, and then said, "I wasn't one of those, Dee. I wasn't one of those who liked to kill. I had to in order to survive, but I didn't like it. I'd get ill after-ward. With each life I took, a little bit of me died, too, but I took comfort in that. I even welcomed those small deaths of mine. At least it let me know that I was still a decent person." Clarence shook his head and looked away.

Dee wished he would put an arm around her, but he made no move to do so, and she felt too shy to make the gesture herself. She would like to be able to offer him comfort, and perhaps, in return, he would comfort her.

She wondered what it would be like to be comforted, to have someone to share her grief with, because she was very tired of bearing it alone. Gran loved her. She knew this. But Gran was never one for kisses or hugs. Even this past week, with Gran so worried about her, they had still been awkward around each other. That was when she realized that perhaps the life she'd planned for herself would be a solitary one. Would she always be alone? Would her life be made up of days that stretched one into the other without anyone to touch or hold?

Her gloomy thoughts made Dee's tongue sharper than she intended. "Where did you go that day? When we found Clooey?" She felt angry that he had abandoned her when she needed him the most, despite knowing she had no hold on Clarence and so no real right to the anger.

"I left you?" Clarence seemed puzzled.

"Yes," Dee said.

He thought for a moment. "I went to check on my family." Then, with certainty. "Yes. I was worried about them. Dee, would you watch out for Vivien? There's something wrong there. She's being secretive of late and that's not like her. She's had such a hard time of it. Grieving over Dad, me gone away to war, and Mother unable to cope and leaving everything for her to do."

Dee felt vaguely ashamed of her uncharitable thoughts about Clarence's sister. Maybe being aloof and apart was Vivien's armour against a world that threatened to overwhelm her. She recalled Gran saying a cloud enveloped Vivien. Perhaps she *should* keep an eye on the girl. But why had Clarence asked her to watch Vivien? Could he not do that himself? Was he planning to go away? Her heart plummeted at the thought.

Clarence continued. "I know you've been at the house. I know you've seen how it is. It wasn't always like that. We had a good home when Dad was alive. Everything changed when he died, but then that's the way of it, isn't it? Things change."

He was right, Dee thought. Everything changes: friends, family, Price's Corners, even her.

"So, if you'd just keep an eye on Vivien for me," Clarence went on.

Dee nodded. "I will. I'd better get home. Gran will be wondering where I am. Clarence, I won't be coming up the mountain for a while." There was, she discovered, little comfort here anymore.

Clarence nodded. "It's probably for the best. It's not safe."

She made her way over the flat rock toward the trees.

"Defiance?"

She turned.

"Do you have a sweetheart?" Clarence asked.

Dee blushed. "No."

"Sorry to be so forward. It's just . . ." he broke off and shook his head sadly. "You should have a sweetheart. If only . . ."

If only, Dee thought, as she pushed through the under-brush to the trail. If only.

CHAPTER SEVENTEEN

The detective arrived from Toronto by automobile. Dee saw him the morning she returned to school. She had dreaded going back, dreaded seeing the empty seat next to her where Clooey had once sat, dreaded it so much that she'd stalled returning for a couple of extra days. Finally, on a Wednesday morning when Dee got up, Gran handed her a large lunch and told her to be off. "Avoiding it isn't going to make it any better," Gran said. "Best to face it head-on."

From her seat in the schoolhouse, Dee saw the detective come out of the police station where he was temporarily staying. A tidy man, small of stature, with a trimmed beard. She watched as he wandered around the village in his brown topcoat and hat, stopping to stare at the church steeple and crossing the street to the Mercantile, looking like he had all the time in the world.

The next day on her way home from school, Dee passed right by him and noted he had a pleasant face, short, light-brown hair, and green eyes behind thick spectacles. He smiled and tipped his hat to her, and Dee could tell he knew all about her, though he said nothing beyond "Good afternoon."

His name was Edwin Hardy and everyone in town was talking about him. Gran said that Mrs. Carter was bustling around the village importantly, buying special cuts of meat "for the Department of Justice detective."

"Not that special cuts will improve her cooking," she added sourly. Mrs. Carter was not in Gran's good books these days, since the constable's wife had put forth her own opinion on who was responsible for the girls' deaths—Gran.

The following few days brought an additional spate of gossip and new interest as everyone speculated about the "detective from Toronto." It was said he had been out to the mill, where he'd questioned a few of the unmarried men, talked to Mr. Richmond, and watched the huge mill machines at work.

He had also been up and down the mountain at least a half dozen times, alone. Everyone wondered when he'd find the murderer.

By the end of the week, Dee found it wasn't as difficult to leave for school. Lugging her bookbag and over-flowing lunch pail—Gran was trying to fatten her up—she headed into the cold November air and down the road, not looking back at the mountain; she never looked at it now. Instead, she glanced over at the old Martin house as she passed, but no one was around. She hadn't seen Clarence since the day he'd asked her to look out for Vivien.

Her hard-soled boots slipped on frozen mud ridges in the road, occasionally breaking through the thin sheet ice that covered water pooled in the wagon ruts. She arrived at Billy's house to find him standing inside his gate, without lunch pail or school books.

"I won't be going to school for a while. Dad wants me near when he's working away from the house. I'm to watch out for Ma and my sisters," he said, pride creeping into his voice at being given such a responsibility.

First no Clooey and now no Billy, but when she got to Podge's, he was waiting in the road just like every morning. Dee found some comfort in the fact that not everything had changed. Today, though, a frown pulled down the corners of his mouth. He kept looking past Dee and back up the road.

"Where's Esther?" he asked.

"I didn't see anyone around their house today," Dee said. "Maybe they're already at school."

"Maybe," Podge said doubtfully.

"Come on or we'll be late." Dee grabbed Podge's hand and gave him a tug toward the schoolhouse. "Look here, Podge. This puddle's frozen. We can slide across it," she said, hoping to distract him.

As she took a run toward the iced-over puddle she fought back an uneasy *feeling*. Where were Vivien and Esther, and the boys? There hadn't been any activity around the house, and now that she thought about it, she hadn't seen any smoke coming out of the chimney this morning either. Surely they hadn't moved on. Surely Clarence would have come over and said goodbye if the family were planning to leave. Distressed, Dee realized she might never see him again. She blinked them back. Silly to cry over a boy you barely know, she chided herself.

As she and Podge neared the school, Dee saw Dr. Hughes's gleaming automobile in the centre of an admiring cluster of students. Chief O'Brien's automobile was parked next to it. Dee's stomach lurched.

Charlie Price saw Dee and came running. "Dee! Chief O'Brien is looking for you. He and Constable Carter and that detective are in there talking to Miss Hamilton right now." His eyes were round with excitement. "He's looking for Podge, too."

"Why?" Dee asked.

"I don't know. He won't say, and Miss Hamilton said we were all to stay outside until she called us in. Except you and Podge. You're both to go in right away."

Dee hesitated and briefly considered turning her feet back down the road the way she'd come. Instead, she took a deep breath. There was nothing for it but to go and see why the chief wanted her.

Aware of everyone's eyes on her, Dee walked slowly toward the schoolhouse stairs. "They're going to arrest her," she heard a boy say. "Maybe they'll take her to jail in the automobile."

"Lucky duck, getting to ride in a motor vehicle," another voice said.

Dee recognized that voice. It was one of Vivien's brothers. So they hadn't left the village.

They wouldn't take her away, would they? She hadn't done anything. Except, maybe it was like Mrs. Carter said, and they were taking her away because they thought she was a witch. Would they burn her? No. They mostly just hanged people nowadays.

Heart beating painfully, she walked up the steps and past a newspaper man who stared curiously at her. They were everywhere these days, these newspaper men, like crows scavenging around the village, poking at the townspeople to get tidbits of news.

She had to turn back once and urge Podge to follow her. "Come on," she said. "Teacher wants to see you."

Podge stopped at the bottom of the steps. He knew he wasn't welcome in the schoolroom. If the teacher wanted to see him, it had to be about something bad.

"I'll be right with you," Dee assured him.

Reluctantly, he followed her, so closely he stepped on Dee's heels. She could feel his heavy breathing hot on her neck and knew he was scared. So was she.

"Here they are," Miss Hamilton said.

Chief O'Brien and Detective Hardy turned to look at them, and that's when Dee saw Esther and Vivien on each side of Miss Hamilton. The teacher had an arm around the younger girl's shoulders. Behind her, Dr. Hughes perched on the edge of the teacher's desk, hands clasped around one bent knee. Constable Carter moved behind Dee and Podge to stand at the entrance to the schoolroom, blocking an escape.

Miss Hamilton suddenly pulled Esther into her skirt. "I always knew he was dangerous. That's why I wouldn't let him in the schoolhouse. As I always said, there is no place for the feeble-minded among normal folk. He should be locked up. You're a very lucky girl that nothing happened to you."

Esther pulled away. "Podge is my friend. He wouldn't hurt me."

Constable Carter stepped forward and grabbed Podge's arm. Alarmed, Podge took a step backwards, his free hand coming up in a fist. The constable pulled out his baton and raised it above his head, preparing to bring it down.

"No need for that," Chief O'Brien said firmly. "There are women and girls present."

The baton lowered, but the constable kept it at the ready.

"What's the matter? What's happening?" Dee asked.

"That retard was going to hurt my sister," Vivien said.

"No, he wasn't." Esther was in tears.

"He was going to take her up the mountain and murder her just like he did Clooey," Vivien said.

"Defiance," Detective Hardy said quietly. "This girl here, Vivien, says you have something from the murder scene of Mary Ann Simpson."

"I don't have anything," Dee said.

"Yes, you do," Vivien broke in. "A carving. Like this one." In the palm of her hand, Vivien held a small wooden bird.

"Podge gave Esther this, and it's just like the one I found under that tree; the murder tree where that other girl's bones were found. You took it away from me. You put it in your pocket."

Dee shrugged, trying to look unconcerned. "Podge carves them all the time. He's given me lots. He gives them to everyone. He probably just dropped it up there." She instantly realized her mistake. "Or I might have dropped it, or someone else," she finished hurriedly.

"You see?" Constable Carter spit in his excitement. "I told you that idiot boy did it. I knew all along he murdered those girls."

"You poor child, you could have been killed by that monster." Miss Hamilton made to embrace Esther again, but the girl pulled away.

"I hate you, Vivien," Esther screeched.

"Enough!" Chief O'Brien held up his hand and waited for them to quiet down. "Dee, this girl says she found one of

Podge's carvings underneath the spruce where we found Mary Ann's bones, and that you took it from her. Is that true?"

Dee looked from face to face, stricken. If she admitted it was true, Podge would be in trouble, but if she disputed Vivien's story, she'd be the one in a mess.

"Yes," she said miserably. "But Podge would never hurt anyone. You've known him a long time, Constable Carter, and you know he'd never hurt a soul."

"I know his sort can't be trusted. Their brains don't work properly," Constable Carter said.

"Evil killed Mary Ann and Clooey, and Podge doesn't have an evil bone in his body," Dee said hotly.

"Evil," the detective echoed softly.

"I put her in your special place where you and Mary Ann used to play, Dee. I put Mary Ann there because she was lonely," Podge said.

Everyone stared at him. Dee felt the temperature plunge in the room, then an incredible wave of heat blasted over her face. At the side of the cloakroom she saw the black pillar rise and swirl toward them, made bold in its triumph. Dee stared at the police officers' faces. Could no one else see? Podge could, Dee realized, seeing the terror on his face; he could *see* the pillar.

"No." She shook her head. It was hard to get the words out; the heat seared her lips. "No. He didn't murder her. Podge must have found Mary Ann after she was killed and moved her. He wouldn't understand that she was dead. He probably thought she was sleeping."

"I'm sorry, Dee, I really am. But he as much as admitted it," Chief O'Brien said. "I'm going to have to take him to the police house for questioning."

Tears streamed down Podge's face. "Mary Ann was sad. She didn't like being all alone. So I moved her under the tree. I knew you'd find her there, Dee."

Constable Carter poked him with his baton and urged him toward the door.

Podge began howling. "Dee! Dee! I'm scared."

"Dr. Hughes," Dee pleaded. "You've seen other people like Podge. Tell them he's harmless."

Dr. Hughes stood up and pulled on his gloves. "I've examined the bones of Mary Ann Simpson and the body of Clooey and reported on how the girls died. That's all I can do. The rest is up to the police."

Dee stood at the top of the schoolhouse steps and watched as Constable Carter yanked Podge toward the police house across the street, his baton wavering above Podge's head. By now a crowd had gathered, drawn by the automobiles and the children gathered outside the schoolhouse. They all stood silent, watching as Podge was led past them. The only people making noise, asking questions, were three newspaper reporters who had descended on the schoolhouse and street like hounds sniffing blood.

"I want my ma!" Podge cried.

Chief O'Brien turned around. "Someone tell Podge's mother we're taking him to the police house. She can meet us there."

Dee grabbed Detective Hardy's arm as he started down the stairs. "You have to believe me, sir. He didn't do it."

"We found another carving. In the dirt near where Clooey was buried." Detective Hardy gently unclasped her fingers. "We're just going to talk to your friend." He followed the others across the street, pushing through the newsmen.

Dee turned to see Vivien standing at the schoolhouse door, a smile on her lips.

"I wish you'd never come here," Dee said.

"Other people think he did it, too. Not just me," Vivien said. "And I found the carving."

"And to think I promised Clarence I'd keep an eye on you."

"Clarence?" Vivien repeated. "What are you talking about?"

Dee went on without listening to her. "But I'm breaking that promise. And I'm never coming back to this school." That was for Miss Hamilton, who stood next to Vivien.

Dee stalked off, legs shaking. She'd go home to Gran, but first she would stop off at Podge's house and break the news to his mother.

CHAPTER EIGHTEEN

Instead of going home as she'd planned, Dee followed Podge's heartbroken mother back to the police house. It had been dreadful telling Mrs. Holmes Podge was in trouble, especially since Dee felt responsible for putting him there. She had to do something to make it right. Positioning herself behind a tree opposite the police house, Dee watched the comings and goings in the village. Evening fell and she saw the electric lights go on in Simpsons' Mercantile, but still she waited in the shadow of the tree trunk, cold and hungry, unable to give up her vigil, despite knowing that Gran would be worried about her.

Another hour passed and the Mercantile lights went off. Dee saw the shadow of Mr. Simpson through the window as he locked the front door, then the lights go on in the living quarters upstairs. Finally, Mrs. Holmes came out of the police house and hurried down the road toward home. Even from a distance, Dee could see the woman's distress. Podge was all she had. Dee stamped her feet to warm them and continued to wait. She was rewarded a few minutes later when Detective Hardy exited the police house. She had been waiting for him.

He stopped on the wooden walk to pull on his gloves, stood and glanced at the starry sky, then lowered his head and stared at the exact spot where Dee was hidden. She slowly stepped away from the tree's shadow and into the street, legs stiff from cold.

"You must have been waiting a long time," Detective Hardy said.

Dee shrugged. "Podge is my friend." Her teeth chattered.

"Let's walk a bit," Detective Hardy suggested. "It will warm you up."

Dee fell in step beside the detective.

"You had a question for me?" He glanced at her face.

"What's going to happen to Podge—George—now?" Dee asked.

"Your chief and constable are sure he is the killer, so they are going to charge him with murder. Doctors will examine him, and there will be a decision as to whether or not he is fit to stand trial."

"And if he isn't?"

The detective sighed. "He'll be sent to a home for the incurables."

"Podge would hate that," Dee cried. "He loves the mountain. He'll die locked up! And if he is found fit and found guilty, they'll hang him, won't they? So it doesn't matter what happens; Podge will never live here again!"

"I am sorry. Either way, it doesn't look good for him," Detective Hardy said. "It's a tragedy for everyone. A crime like this doesn't just affect the families involved, it tears entire towns apart."

"But he didn't do it. Podge is too shy to even talk to girls my age, except me. He wouldn't know to do . . ." Dee hesitated. "To do *that* with them."

Detective Hardy raised his eyebrows.

"I've helped my grandmother deliver babies," Dee said flatly. "I know young ladies aren't supposed to *know* about stuff like that, but I do."

"You must give Mrs. Carter a run for her money," Detective Hardy said. He gave a soft chuckle.

"She doesn't like me or Gran too much," Dee confided.

"She's a woman to be contended with, I will agree. And an abominable cook. Truth be told, I'm escaping her dinner meal right now," Detective Hardy told her.

Dee smiled, appreciating that he was trying to be kind and distract her from Podge's fate, but her heart was broken. They left the village and walked past Cissy's place.

"It's all Vivien's fault. If she hadn't opened her mouth, Podge would be home right now."

"Now there is an interesting young woman," Detective Hardy said. "To all appearances, I wouldn't have thought she would have the intelligence to connect the carving to the murderer. So I understand she found it first in the dirt under the tree, and you took it from her and put it in your pocket?"

"Yes," Dee admitted. "I just thought Podge had been there and dropped it. I guess I knew it wouldn't be good for him if Chief O'Brien had found it near where Mary Ann's bones were found. I shouldn't have hidden it. I know that. But he didn't do it. It's not Podge. If it was, I would have . . ." She broke off, fearing she'd said too much.

"*Known?*" The detective stopped walking and turned to her.

Dee decided to throw caution to the wind. She was tired of secrets and hiding all the time. She was who she was. "Yes. I would have *known*. Gran and I, we're different. Gran sometimes knows what is going to happen, well, before it happens, and she knows what ills a person has by looking at him, and I—I can see the spirits of dead people. And I can tell how a person died. Sort of," she added. "It's not *all* revealed. It comes in bits and pieces, like a jigsaw puzzle, and I have to put it together. Gran says many people have the same skills as us; that is what she calls them, skills, but they just don't use that part of themselves."

"And you *know* your friend is not guilty?" Detective Hardy said.

"Yes. I don't *feel* anything bad from Podge. But the problem is, I don't know who is bad. I can't *see* or *feel* who killed the girls."

Dee paused for a moment. "Detective Hardy, ask Podge himself. Ask him if he killed Mary Ann or Clooey. I don't think Podge knows how to lie. That's why he told Chief O'Brien that he had moved Mary Ann's body. He told him the truth."

They continued up the road, and Dee realized he was walking her home.

"You don't think Podge is guilty either," she said suddenly. "If you did, you wouldn't be walking me to my house."

Detective Hardy smiled. "You are very perceptive, Miss Vale. I actually do not think your young friend is guilty. Let's just say it's my own *feeling*."

Dee stopped in her tracks. "Then you can let him out of jail."

"Unfortunately, until there is someone else to take his place, I can't. Or sadly, until another girl is murdered. He couldn't do that if he's locked up. That's the problem with detaining a suspect who isn't the killer. People will lower their vigilance, and whoever is doing this will not stop. And he'll feel safer now believing we have the murderer. I fear it will happen again, and soon."

"Why does he keep killing?" asked Dee.

"I don't know," Detective Hardy said. "Maybe someday people will find the answer as to why there are people like this murderer. Perhaps there is something wrong in their brains." The detective shrugged.

"It's evil," Dee said flatly.

"Yes, there is that. Doing what I do, you soon believe in evil. It has a distinct—" he paused looking for a suitable word, "—presence. My belief is that the person committing these crimes is just a vessel to be used by evil. But there must be a reason why that particular person is selected—a weakness of character, selfishness perhaps, or a predisposition to do wrong."

"Gran says that evil disguises itself."

"Yes, that has been my experience also, but make no mistake, young lady, I will find it out," Detective Hardy said. "That aside, at this point, your friend Podge, as you call him, is probably safer in the police house than at his own home. Emotions are running very high in the area."

They had arrived at her gate.

"Why does the killer bury them in the same place?" Dee asked. "Why not put them in different spots so it would be more difficult for the police to find them?"

Detective Hardy leaned against the fence and crossed his arms. "The criminal mind is very complicated. I have discovered that the murderer is drawn back to the scene of his crime again and again; he's compelled to return. Sometimes I think he is checking to see if anyone has found the result of his handiwork, and other times, it's to relive the crime. There is even sometimes impatience involved. The killer wonders why no one has found him out. He believes himself more intelligent than those around him, and, with each subsequent murder, he becomes bolder. He'll even pretend to help the police, while all the time he thinks he is smarter than them."

"So that's why you keep going up the mountain," Dee said.

"I hadn't realized my movements were so closely monitored, but yes, that's one of the reasons I go."

He glanced at the intimidating shadow of the mountain. "So you didn't *feel* anything at the graves on the mountain?"

"I felt their pain and their fear." Dee caught her breath in a sob. "But not their deaths."

"I'm sorry," Detective Hardy said. "It is quite a burden you live with, to feel other peoples' horror, and doubly so when they are your friends."

"If only I could *see* who did it!" Dee cried.

"I will leave you here, Miss Vale," Detective Hardy said. He gently patted her arm. "Perhaps when this is all over, you and your grandmother and I can have a talk. I don't think we are all that different. A lot of my work involves *hunches*, you might call them. I'm not returning home for a few days. I will be continuing to conduct my investigation." He sighed and stared up at the sky. "It's very peaceful here. Not like the city. All those soldiers back from the war, with time on their hands, they're keeping us police officers busy."

They both peered at the night sky for a moment. Then the

detective went on. "Constable Carter will be by tomorrow morning to take your statement about finding the carving. In the meantime, should you have any questions or *hunches*, please do not hesitate to come and see me. And, Miss Vale, take care. Do not go out alone, especially not to your beloved mountain. I do not think this is over."

CHAPTER NINETEEN

Dee left the detective and went into the house, prepared for a tongue-lashing, only to find Gran hurriedly packing her birthing bag. "I'm glad you're here," was all she said.

"What's the matter?" asked Dee.

"There's a baby wanting to be born the other side of the village ..."

Dee nodded. Gran must mean the smithy's wife, Mrs. Shaw. She'd had a difficult pregnancy.

"And Cissy's not well. She sent one of the children to ask us to come."

"Not Ray? The children shouldn't be out this late," Dee said.

"I guess he's not home. Which will make your work easier," Gran replied.

"My work?" Dee repeated.

"Mr. Shaw will soon be here to pick me up, so listen carefully. You need to give Cissy tansy tea if we're going to save her and that baby," Gran told. "There's very little else you can do other than keep Cissy's legs raised and, most importantly, keep her in bed."

"But shouldn't you be there?" Dee stammered. She'd never taken care of an expectant mother on her own.

"I can't be in two places at one time. Mrs. Shaw is too old to be having a baby. I really would prefer if she had the doctor attend her, but she refuses. Cissy is younger and stronger. I'll see to Mrs. Shaw and then I'll come directly to Cissy. I'll leave word for Dr. Hughes to come as soon as possible. You'll have to manage by yourself until then." Gran stopped packing and caught Dee's eye. "You'll be fine, and Cissy appreciates your company. She says you have a way of making her feel better. Now, make up a package of tea. I'll have Mr. Shaw drop you off on our way into Price's Corners."

Dee didn't move right away. "Gran, something horrible happened today."

"I know," Gran said gently. "Why don't you tell me about it while you get ready?"

As Dee packed a small case for herself, she told Gran all about Podge being taken to the police house and what Detective Hardy had told her about the murderer.

"I don't want you wandering around on your own until this is over," Gran said. "I am sorry about Podge. I don't know what his mother will do without him."

A horse and wagon pulled up at their gate and they quickly went down the walk. Dee suddenly stopped. "Should we lock the door?"

"No, I put a spell on the place," Gran said.

Dee blinked.

"I did not really, Granddaughter," Gran said. She walked quickly to the gate. Dee followed, still amazed that her grandmother had made a joke.

Mr. Shaw scrambled down and helped Gran and Dee into the wagon.

"But I will not start locking my doors," Gran continued. "That is the beginning. Where will our fear take us then? Will we burn down the houses of people we fear? Or do worse? That is the way evil is born. We must fight it any way we can."

They arrived at Cissy's to find their way barred by an intoxicated Ray Price. "I will not have a witch and her bastard granddaughter in my house," he shouted. He swayed on his feet, and from where she stood behind her grandmother, Dee could smell whiskey fumes.

A baby's angry cries came from the kitchen, and Dee could hear the fearful whimpers of the other children. What was more worrisome was the metallic smell that permeated the air. Blood.

"Let Dee in, or your wife's death will be on your head," Gran said. "And then who will take care of these children? You?"

Ray stared at her blearily. "I'll get Dr. Hughes. A real doctor."

"I'm heading into town now. I will send a message from the police house for the doctor to come. Dee will stay with Cissy until he can get here," Gran said. "I'll just do a quick check of Cissy before I go on with Mr. Shaw." She went into the bedroom and shut the door.

Dee pushed past Ray and hurried over to the cradle to pick up the baby. She gave her little finger for the baby to suck on, in an attempt to soothe her. The children huddled around the table, faces pale, eyes wide, a couple of the younger ones with tear tracks down their cheeks.

"Have you had any supper?" Dee asked.

They shook their heads.

That would be the first thing to take care of while Gran saw to Cissy. Get some food into the children and into Ray, if he'd take any. It would make the children drowsy and ready for bed and hopefully soak up some of the alcohol Ray had consumed. Dee drenched the corner of a clean towel in milk and gave the baby to the oldest girl, telling her to let the baby suck on the fabric. She cut a crust of bread and gave it to the crying toddler, then set a frying pan on the stove. She filled the kettle from the pump and set it beside the skillet to boil.

"We need wood," she told Ray, trying to put her gran's tone of authority into her own voice, though her legs wobbled beneath her.

It seemed to work, as he grabbed one of the boys by the arm and dragged him outside with him. A few minutes later the boy stumbled in with an armload of wood. Dee could hear the sounds of chopping. She just hoped Ray didn't chop off his foot in his drunken condition, but she didn't worry about that for too long. She was more concerned about Cissy.

Gran came out of the bedroom and washed her hands in a pan in the sink. "She's going to lose the baby," she whispered to Dee. "All you can do is sit with her and keep her comfortable. I'll be back as soon as I can." She dried her hands and left.

Dee quickly scooped grease into the now-hot frying pan and added chopped potatoes and onions. It might not be fancy, she thought, but it would be filling. She sliced bread and put it out with jam she found in the pantry. The children's eyes lit up, and Dee realized they probably got jam only on special occasions.

Now to see to Cissy. "Keep an eye on that pan," she told another of the girls. "And keep the babies away from the hot stove. I'll be right back."

She went into the bedroom and closed the door behind her. The sickly scent of blood filled her nostrils, and she could taste it at the back of her throat. Alarmed, she raised the blanket covering Cissy's legs, then quickly lowered it.

Cissy rolled her head, clearly in pain.

"It's me, Cissy," Dee said. "I'm going to try to make you more comfortable. I'll be right back."

Gently closing the bedroom door behind her, she went into the kitchen. The boiling kettle spat hissing drops onto the stove. Dee poured the hot water over the tea leaves she'd brought with her from home. She prayed it would work. Cissy had lost a lot of blood. While she waited for the tea to steep, she spooned the potatoes and onions onto the children's plates, after which she thoroughly washed her hands, like Gran had taught her. Half of all blood infections, Gran said, came from the person helping rather than from the illness itself.

As she dried her hands, Ray lurched into the kitchen, a chunk of wood dangling from one hand, an axe from the other. "What's going on?" he asked suspiciously.

Surprised at her own assurance, Dee steered Ray back onto the porch. She didn't want the children to overhear them speaking. "Cissy is in a bad way. She's miscarrying and losing a lot of blood. There's nothing I can do for the baby. It's too young. It will be born dead. I'm going to try to save Cissy. I'll do what I can until Dr. Hughes or Gran get here."

It was a real possibility that Cissy could die. Women passed on in child birth all the time. What would Dee do without the woman's gentleness to take the harshness from her own life? Who else would share Mama with her?

"We'll need a lot of wood for the night," Dee finished. She hoped chopping it would keep Ray out from underfoot.

Back in the bedroom, Dee gently washed Cissy's face and held her hand when pain ripped through the woman. In the calmer moments, Dee held a cup of the brewed tea to Cissy's lips, trying hard to not let Cissy see how her hands trembled.

She left a few times to see that the children ate their supper and to supervise their going to bed. Later, she went out to refresh the tea and found Ray sitting in a chair near the stove, head on his chest, snoring.

There wasn't a clock in the bedroom, so Dee didn't know how many hours passed while she sat with Cissy. Finally, the baby slipped out, and Dee wrapped the tiny, still body in a blanket and handed him to Cissy to hold and cry over. Some people thought it not proper for the mother to see her dead baby, but Gran said it was a part of mourning. You needed something to hold on to, and then to be able to put away from you, to begin to grieve. By now Dee was shaking from head to foot with fatigue and nerves. She was also very worried about the amount of blood still leaking from Cissy. She packed a towel between Cissy's legs to stem the flow. It had to be stopped and she was at her wit's end to know what else she could do.

She heard the front door bang open and Dr. Hughes and Gran rushed into the bedroom.

Dr. Hughes asked Dee to bring water and clean towels. Relieved to have the responsibility taken out of her hands, she rushed to do his bidding. She watched as he removed the towels from Cissy's legs. "You did a good job here," he said to Dee.

Gran took the stillborn baby from Cissy, covered its face, and went out into the kitchen. A minute later, Dee heard Ray cursing and Gran's voice raised. Then all was quiet.

"Hold Mrs. Price's hand," Dr. Hughes ordered Dee. "I need her still while I stitch her up."

Dee went to the head of the bed and grasped Cissy's hand. It was cold and clammy. Cissy's white face was framed by the stark black of her hair spread across the pillow. Scared, Dee closed her eyes and tried to direct warmth through her hand into Cissy's pale face. After a little while, she opened her eyes and saw a bit of colour staining Cissy's cheeks.

"Thank you," Cissy whispered.

Dee smiled shakily and squeezed Cissy's hand until the doctor finished.

He stood up and bent over Cissy, putting an ear to the woman's chest. He listened a moment, then straightened. "She's sleeping now. Best thing for her," he said.

Dee followed him into the kitchen, shutting the bedroom door behind her.

"You kept your head about you," Dr. Hughes told Dee as he washed and dried his hands. "I can see why your granddaughter wants to be a nurse," he continued to her grandmother.

Gran raised her eyebrows at Dee, who flushed and turned away. Gran wouldn't like hearing that her granddaughter wanted to be a nurse from someone other than Dee. But all she said was, "She has a gentle touch."

Dr. Hughes packed up his bag. "If you want to drop by my office next time you are in Wallen, Dee, I can lend you some medical books to read to help you get started if you decide nursing is what you want to pursue."

"Thank you," Dee said.

"You're a smart girl, determined too. A lot like your mother was at your age," he went on.

"I didn't realize you knew my daughter so well," Gran interrupted quietly.

To anyone else it might have seemed a casual comment, but Dee could hear an edge to her grandmother's voice.

"I didn't. I saw her around town, going to school, at the store. Like I see Dee here and all the other children." Dr. Hughes snapped his bag shut and pulled on his coat. "You'll stay the night? Mrs. Price is going to need a lot of rest in the coming days."

"We'll both stay until Cissy doesn't need us anymore," Gran assured him.

Dee sank into a chair, utterly exhausted.

"I'll take the infant's body with me to town and let the minister know. He'll contact you, Mr. Price, about the burying. It's a shame, but at least the mother survived. I saw so much death overseas during the war, but it's still a babe's death that bothers me most." He shook his head. "I'll stop by tomorrow to see how she's doing."

Dee felt her eyes begin to close.

"Granddaughter, get some fresh sheets," Gran ordered.

Wearily, Dee pulled herself from the chair and found clean linen in Cissy's drying cupboard. She and her grandmother gently rolled Cissy over and changed the dirty bedclothes beneath her.

"I'm sorry, Gran," Dee said quietly, not wanting to wake Cissy. She wanted to explain about nursing, but Gran stopped her.

"Nurses are nothing more than servants in those hospitals," she whispered. "You'll be doing the lowliest of jobs and there'll be no thanks given you."

"Dr. Hughes says it's changing. Some nurses don't even work in hospitals but go to the small towns and the countryside and help people. Like Cissy here. It scared me, Gran, that Cissy was so ill and I didn't know what to do. If I'd had training, I would have known."

"You did very well," Gran said. She bent, tucking in the corner of a sheet beneath the mattress. Dee felt surprise first, then a warmth spread over her. It wasn't often that Gran praised her.

"I don't want you being ordered about by some male doctor who doesn't know as much as you do," Gran went on.

Dee smiled wryly. Like she'd been ordered around by Gran all her life? But she wisely decided not to say anything.

"You seem to be talking a lot with Dr. Hughes," Gran said.

Dee carefully spread a blanket over Cissy, who was fast asleep. "I saw him at the store recently and asked him about being a pupil nurse. It's what I'd really like to do, Gran. Clarence, he said that overseas the nurses were the ones saving lives, not just the doctors. He said nurses were a godsend to the soldiers."

"Clarence?" Gran asked, puzzled.

Dee realized what she'd said. Well, there was nothing for it but to own up to all her misdeeds. "Vivien's older brother. I met him up the mountain and we were talking. I know it's a bit forward to see a boy on my own, but he's really nice, Gran, and . . ."

A crash, followed by a child's cry, came from the kitchen. Startled, they both turned toward the door. "I'll finish up here. You go and put that youngster back to bed," Gran said. And there was no more talk of Clarence.

Later that night, as Dee lay in bed between two of Cissy's daughters, she thought about her long day. She was so tired, but her mind just wouldn't let her rest. First, there was Podge. She wondered how he was doing at the police house. There wouldn't be much comfort given him by the Carters. She rolled over onto her side and thought about the murders. On her fingers she counted the years between the deaths of Mary Ann and Clooey. There was a four-year gap; a four-year gap between Mary Ann's death and Clooey's, but the previous girls had all gone missing within a year or so of each other.

So why were there no killings in those four years? What had happened in those four years? The answer suddenly came to her. The war. Many of the men in Price's Corners had been overseas during those four years. And whoever had killed Clooey had been among them. As she fell into sleep, Dee wondered if she should tell Detective Hardy. Or would he just think her a foolish, young girl? In her gut, though, she knew she was right.

CHAPTER TWENTY

After a couple of days of rest, Cissy was feeling better, and Gran asked Dee to walk the children to school, saying she could care for Cissy on her own for a while. Dee knew what her grandmother was doing and she didn't like it one bit. Gran thought that once Dee went to the schoolhouse, she'd realize how much she missed it and would want to go back. Well, Gran could think again, Dee told herself heatedly. School only meant loss to her now: Clooey, Billy, and Podge. She'd walk the children to the schoolhouse door and turn right around.

Her breath puffed white in the cold November air. One of the Price boys jumped and broke through the ice on top of a puddle, splashing brown mud over Dee's stockings. She yelled at him to stop, but he laughed and did it again.

"I pity the woman who marries you!" Dee yelled.

The children ran ahead and Dee made no attempt to keep up. She couldn't think with them chattering anyway. The only good thing about having six children underfoot was that there hadn't been one spare minute for her and Gran to talk, about nursing—or Clarence. Granted, there were times when Dee was mad that her grandmother wouldn't talk, but this wasn't one of them.

In the light of day, Dee had decided not to tell Detective Hardy about her notion that the killer was a returning soldier. He was a great detective, so he probably had already thought of it. But that didn't mean she couldn't think about it herself. She mulled over the names of those who had gone away from Price's Corners—and returned: Billy's father, Constable Carter, Reverend MacAllister, Mister, and all the men from the mill who she didn't know. Ray Price had a heart problem that had kept him home, and Mr. Richmond and Mr. Simpson had been too old to sign up, so none of them could be the killer.

And of those who had come back, Clooey's father was too ill to leave the house, and Constable Carter—well, he would do only what Mrs. Carter told him to do, and for all her faults, Dee couldn't see the woman telling him to murder someone. Reverend MacAllister was a man of the cloth, so it was doubtful that he would have blood on his hands.

The men from the mill, she couldn't say one way or the other about them, and the same went for the men from Wallen who had served, except for Dr. Hughes, and he was a doctor. He saved lives, he didn't take them. Her brain was tired from going round and round, but the only thing she knew for sure was that Podge had not done it.

As Dee entered the village, she saw women going into Mr. Simpson's store, and the schoolyard was full. No one was keeping their children home anymore. The entire town seemed lighter, a weight lifted off them now that Podge was in jail. Ray Price had come home the day before to tell them that a trial date had been set for the first week of December—in two weeks' time. The doctors who had examined Podge had found him competent, as he knew right from wrong. Ray had gone on to say that Podge's mother had sold her house to pay for a lawyer to defend Podge and was now living in her own house as a tenant. Gran had just shaken her head at the news.

As Dee made her way around a knot of men who stood in front of the livery, she heard one say, "Perfect timing for a trial; harvest's all in."

"I'm taking the wife," another said. "She's making up a picnic lunch. Have to get there early, though, as they're expecting huge crowds."

Most of the businesses in Price's Corners and some in Wallen were closing for the day of the trial, while other more canny storeowners in Wallen were staying open, hoping to profit from the expected large turnout. Dee had heard that the hotel in Wallen had hired extra wait staff for the lunch and dinner hours.

Cissy's children safely in the schoolyard, Dee crossed the street to the police house. She'd go and visit Podge. He'd be very lonely and missing his friends. Of course, it would mean facing Mrs. Carter.

Nervously, Dee knocked on the police house door. Maybe Detective Hardy would answer. The door opened and Dee's heart sank. It was Mrs. Carter.

"I'd like to see Podge, please," Dee said politely.

Mrs. Carter pursed her mouth. "The very idea. A young girl cavorting with a criminal. It's unseemly."

"It's just Podge. I've seen him every day of my life," Dee argued.

"I would be remiss in my duties if I allowed you in to see him." Mrs. Carter closed the door firmly.

"And he's not a criminal. He's innocent," Dee yelled at the shut door. But Mrs. Carter didn't come back.

Dee stood on the road in front of the police house, disheartened and uncertain of what to do next.

"Won't the head of the Fussy Society let you in?" Clarence came up beside her.

Dee's heart leapt. She had thought she might never see him again.

"No." Dee stomped her foot. "It's unseemly, she says. Podge must be so lonely and scared. They're having a trial the first week of December. They say he murdered both Mary Ann and Clooey."

"I'm sorry," Clarence said. "Is there any way he could have done it, even accidentally?"

Dee thought it over.

"No," she said. "He's always so gentle." As she said this, she realized she was certain Podge had nothing to do with the deaths. No doubts lingered.

She and Clarence watched the children playing.

"Aren't you going to school?" Clarence asked.

"No," Dee told him. "I'm so mad at Miss Hamilton. I can't believe she told everyone Podge was a murderer."

"You'll never be a nurse if you don't go to school," Clarence pointed out.

"I know," Dee sighed.

"Just swallow your pride, Defiance," Clarence said gently. "It will only be awkward for the first while, and then it will all be over. Tomorrow no one will even remember you yelling at the teacher."

"You're right," Dee said.

"I'm a man. Mrs. Carter can't stop me. I'll go and visit Podge," Clarence said. "I'll tell him you tried to see him."

Feeling a bit more cheerful, Dee dodged a wagon and ran across the street to the schoolhouse. Once there, she turned to wave at Clarence, but he was gone. Dee couldn't believe he'd persuaded Mrs. Carter that fast! It must be nice to be a man, she thought ruefully.

She sat on the bottom step of the schoolhouse waiting for

Miss Hamilton to ring the bell to start classes. Shredding a piece of red ribbon, leftover decoration from the Armistice Day dance earlier in the month, she wondered what she would do if Miss Hamilton wouldn't let her in. What if Miss Hamilton's "no place for the feeble-minded" rule now applied to her, Dee?

A few minutes later, a group of girls, Vivien in the centre of them, gathered at the side of the steps, next to the schoolhouse door, sheltering themselves from the cold wind. This was a new Vivien: animated, clean, and neatly dressed, blonde hair gleaming against the back of a new black coat. Dee wondered where she got it. Certainly her mother couldn't afford a new coat! Her face glowed, except—Dee blinked. A shadow passed over Vivien's face. Then just as quickly, it was gone. Or had it even been there in the first place? Dee couldn't trust what her eyes were seeing anymore.

Vivien was once again telling the story of finding the wooden carving. She had been asked to repeat the tale so often that it came out easily, with no hesitation. Dee sighed. Didn't people ever tire of hearing it?

Dee closed her own ears, until she heard Vivien say excitedly, "I am to testify as a witness at the trial."

"Why?" asked Dee, surprise forcing the question from her. She stood up and faced the girls.

"Because I found the carving that Podge left at the murder scene. You will be testifying, too, Dee, because you took the carving from me and put it in your pocket to hide it. Dr.

Hughes said Constable Carter will be bringing you papers telling you so sometime today."

Dee's heart thumped. Testify? In front of people? She would be asked questions; questions about her *feelings*. And she would have to tell the truth! She'd be up there, in front of everyone, exposed to their stares, their mutters, and their narrow-mindedness. She'd be in front of people who wouldn't understand, who'd either laugh or think her crazy or that she was a tool of the devil. That's what Reverend McAllister had called her once, a tool of the devil. Would they place *her* in a home for the incurables?

"And after the trial is over, and Christmas, I will be leaving school," Vivien went on. "I'm to be employed by Dr. Hughes as a companion to his wife."

"You're going to be the Hughes's maid?" Dee asked.

"A *companion*," Vivien stressed. "I'll be doing a bit of light housework, but mostly I'm to keep Mrs. Hughes company. She has a delicate constitution that keeps her from getting out, and, of course, Dr. Hughes is very busy, so she is alone a lot." Vivien turned to the other girls. "I went to their house for an interview. Mrs. Hughes is a real lady. I'll be reading to her and accompanying her on shopping trips. Dr. Hughes thought that after Christmas would be the best time because . . . because of Clooey. He didn't want anyone taking her place too soon. He gave me this coat so I'd look decent for my new position," she added, running her hands down the coat's front.

Dee cringed at the thought of Vivien taking Clooey's place.

"Mrs. Hughes was asking me about you, Dee," Vivien said. "She asked me if you were nice and if we were friends. Do you know her?"

Before Dee could answer, Miss Hamilton opened the schoolhouse door and rang the handbell. Children scrambled from all corners of the yard to the steps and lined up. Dee went to join them when, to her own surprise, her feet turned right around and marched away from the school. She couldn't face Miss Hamilton. She couldn't face those people at the trial. She didn't know what to do.

Wandering aimlessly down the road, she heard a rumble behind her. Turning her head, she saw that it was Dr. Hughes's automobile. She stepped to the side near the ditch to let him pass, but he stopped beside her.

"I was just going to see Mrs. Price, if you would like a lift," he said.

Dee hesitated a moment, then nodded. She'd been in a motor vehicle only once before and had enjoyed herself immensely. She opened the door and climbed in.

"No school today?" Dr. Hughes asked.

Dee shifted uncomfortably. "Yes, but . . ." She floundered for an acceptable reason for not being in school. "I wasn't feeling too well," she said desperately.

"Oh?" Dr. Hughes raised an eyebrow.

Perhaps telling a doctor you weren't feeling too well wasn't a very good idea, Dee decided too late.

"I think I'm just tired," she explained hurriedly.

"Well, I imagine taking care of all those Price children is quite a bit of work for you and your grandmother," Dr. Hughes said.

"Yes," Dee readily agreed.

She watched the trees speed by, so much faster than in a wagon. If she let her gaze unfocus, the trunks melted into a brown blur.

"You did a wonderful job with Mrs. Price," Dr. Hughes went on. "I think you might have saved her life."

Dee's cheeks turned hot from the praise.

"You haven't come by to pick up any medical books."

"We haven't been to Wallen lately. Though I guess we'll be in town for Podge's trial. Vivien says I'll have to testify."

They drove over a bump that almost jolted Dee out of her seat.

"Sorry about that." Dr. Hughes frowned. "These are hard roads for a motor vehicle. I'm constantly changing flat tires."

After a moment Dee said, "I tried to see Podge today, but Mrs. Carter won't let me. And I'm scared to testify."

Tears pricked her eyes. Dee hoped she wouldn't cry in front of Dr. Hughes and embarrass herself.

"You have to tell the truth."

She nodded. Before long, the automobile pulled up in front of Cissy's house.

"It's an awful business." Dr. Hughes turned off the motor. "Podge is being moved to Wallen jail later today. Detective Hardy will go with him and then home to Toronto."

Dee felt a moment's panic. Detective Hardy was leaving? But he was supposed to find the real murderer! She didn't realize until now how much she'd counted on him being an ally to free Podge. She had seen him passing Cissy's house a couple of times in his automobile, heading for the mountain. Maybe there wasn't any more evidence to be found. Perhaps she should talk to him before he left. She decided to confide in Dr. Hughes. He would know if her notion was worth telling the detective or not.

"Do you think the murderer could be someone who went away to war?" Dee asked timidly.

"Why do you ask that?"

"Well, there were four years when no girls were killed, and then Clooey . . ." She couldn't finish, couldn't actually say out loud that Clooey had been murdered.

Dr. Hughes stroked his moustache. "I guess it's a possibility," he said doubtfully.

Dee knew it. Her idea was dumb. It was a good thing she hadn't said anything to Detective Hardy.

"You shouldn't be worrying about murderers," Dr. Hughes went on. "Leave that to the experts."

Dee climbed out of the car. She guessed he was right. "Thank you very much for the ride," Dee said politely. "It was much better than walking."

Dr. Hughes laughed.

Dee looked despondently at the Price house. "I think I'll go home. To feed Trojan . . ." Her voice trailed off.

Dr. Hughes gathered his bag. "That sounds like a good idea. I don't see any need for me to tell your grandmother about your truancy. Go have a bit of a rest."

"Thank you," Dee said.

She waved goodbye and started to walk toward her house.

"Dee," Dr. Hughes called.

She turned, waited.

"Don't go up the mountain today. Please."

"I won't," she promised.

CHAPTER TWENTY-ONE

The trial for Mary Ann and Clooey's murders was to be held in the Wallen town hall, a two-storey stone building with a soaring bell tower, the only building in town large enough to hold the expected crowds. Dee, Gran, and Mr. Forgetti arrived early on the crisp December morning of the trial, shocked to see huge numbers of people already gathered on the walk outside the hall, jostling each other to get inside. Buggies, wagons, and automobiles lined both sides of the main street as far as the eye could see. Dee's heart thudded. How could she get up in front of all these people? And Podge, he would be overwhelmed.

Constable Carter and another policeman stood on the top steps of the town hall, guarding the wooden double doors. Even from the street, Dee could see that the constable was enjoying himself immensely, deciding who to let into the hall and who to keep out.

"A terrible thing," Mr. Forgetti kept muttering as he drove

the length of the street looking for a place to leave the horses and wagon. Dee was thankful that he had offered to drive her and Gran to the trial, though he said he would not attend "such a terrible thing." He just wanted to be sure Mrs. Vale and her granddaughter got to town and back safe, he said, waving away Gran's thanks. "We help each other, no? That's what friends do."

"Why are all these people here?" Dee asked.

"It's a bit of excitement," Gran explained as Mr. Forgetti helped her down from the wagon seat, having finally found an open spot near the hotel.

"I wait here for you," he said.

"It could be a long time," Gran protested.

"No matter. But I not come in. I don't want to hear." Mr. Forgetti shuddered.

Dee didn't want to hear either, but she had been summoned, as had her grandmother, a surprise to both of them. What on earth could Gran have to tell them? Though, from her grandmother's stony face, Dee had suspicions that Gran knew what was to come. Secrets again.

Constable Carter saw them at the back of the crowd and came down the steps, parting a path with his baton. "Make way for witnesses," he bellowed. "Make way for witnesses."

Dee cringed as all eyes turned toward them. The crowd surged forward, and people craned their necks to see *the witnesses*. A shout from above brought Dee's head up. Two young men hung over the bell tower. Others, she saw, perched on top of telephone poles or sat in the topmost branches of trees to get a better view of the spectacle. Not watching where she was going, Dee tripped on the uneven sidewalk, falling to her knees. She struggled to right herself, but the bodies swept over her, keeping her down. She gasped for air but couldn't find any. She was drowning. Just then, a hand grabbed her and pulled her to her feet.

"If anyone should be considered for the lunatic asylum it should be *that* man," Detective Hardy said, nodding toward Constable Carter. "There is a side door for witnesses to enter and he knows it. Are you hurt?" he asked Dee.

She shook her head. Detective Hardy kept one hand on her elbow, his other helping Dee's grandmother as he pushed through the crowd to the building's side entrance.

Inside, every seat in the large hall was filled. And where they couldn't sit, men and women stood shoulder to shoulder, packed into every square inch.

"Where did they all come from?" Dee whispered.

"Everywhere," Detective Hardy replied. "A special train-load of spectators arrived from Toronto early this morning, and many of those came from even farther afield, as far as the United States. Murder is popular, especially when young girls are involved. These murders have been widely reported in the newspapers, so there is a great deal of interest."

He led them across the front of the room to seats that were

reserved for witnesses. Dee again felt like everyone's eyes were on her, so she kept her head down.

"If you think this is bad," Detective Hardy said, raising his voice slightly to be heard, "you should have seen the numbers that used to come to a hanging. People would bring their children and a picnic lunch for a day's outing. Thank goodness there are no more public spectacles like that allowed."

Dee shuddered.

"It is also interesting to note that even the fairer sex is not immune to morbid curiosity," he continued, referring to the large number of women who had turned out for the trial. "It is a recent trend for women to attend trials, and lately, they have been outnumbering the men. They also seem to relish the less savoury details. I'm not sure how becoming that is to them."

Dee and her grandmother sat down on two chairs beside each other. The seat beside Dee was empty. She darted a quick look around the room. The ceiling soared up two storeys, with an upper balcony on three sides overlooking the hall. People leaned far over the carved wooden railing, yelling to those below. Dee hoped no one would fall in all the excitement. Every few feet along the walls were electric-light sconces.

Ahead of her a raised dais held three ornate chairs, like thrones, Dee thought, over which a picture of King George V in full regalia hung. A table stood in front of the chairs. To each side of and facing the dais more chairs had been set out, as if for a choir in a church. Tables ran the length of these chairs with the exception of a small cleared space to Dee's left. A policeman stood there, guarding it.

"That is the dock—" Detective Hardy pointed to the clearing in front of the stage, enclosed by wooden rails, "—where the prisoner will be."

Poor Podge, Dee thought. To be called a prisoner and put on display for all to see.

"The centre chair on the platform is where the chief justice will sit to preside over the proceedings, flanked by his secretaries. And the chairs on the right side are for the crown attorney and the prisoner's defence lawyer. The row of chairs is for the jury." Detective Hardy patted Dee's shoulder. "I will be seated at the end of the row if you need anything. You will do fine. Just tell the truth."

Tell the truth. . . . Dee's stomach knotted with anxiety. The room was incredibly hot, heated by all the bodies. She removed her scarf from about her neck but kept her wool hat and Sunday coat on. They were her armour, protecting her from the view of the crowd. She couldn't see them behind her, but she could feel their stares and occasionally heard her name spoken. Gran sat tall beside her, staring straight ahead.

From behind them came the sound of muffled sobs and Dee knew without turning that it was Podge's mother. Clooey's mother would be here, too, she realized, as would Mr. and Mrs. Simpson. So many lives touched, so much sorrow caused, all from one person's terrible deeds. But would he know that? Or would he even care?

"Hey, Miss. Miss. Look this way," a voice called.

Without thinking, Dee raised her head and a flash went off in her face. A photographer. Why would they want a picture of her?

Gran's gloved hand reached over and covered Dee's, squeezed it comfortingly.

Dee took her cue from her grandmother and stared at the bunting strung across the stage and around the room. This hall, too, had seen an Armistice Day dance on November 11, with music and laughter. But, today, the walls would recoil from the horror of the recounting of two young girls' death. It was just a room, Dee reminded herself. It had no say in which dramas played out in it.

A rustle of cloth and Vivien, in her new black coat, sat down next to Dee. Cheeks flushed with colour, her pale eyes shot around the room. "Isn't this exciting?" she whispered.

Dee didn't answer. Her spirits rose a bit as she wondered if Clarence had brought his sister to the trial. Even now he might be standing at the back of the room. Dee fought the impulse to turn around to see.

The bell in the tower tolled ten o'clock. The crown attorney walked in, followed by his assistants, carrying large boxes. They were followed by the defence lawyer and his staff. A short delay and the twenty men who made up the jury filed in and took their seats. The room quieted and a portly, stern-looking man entered, trailed by two younger men carrying papers. Everyone stood as these officials climbed two steps up onto the platform and settled themselves on the throne-like chairs at the front. Only then did people sit back down.

The secretaries spread out their papers and took out pens and ink in preparation for the trial.

"I am Chief Justice Randolph Brimwell from the City of Toronto. We are here today to conduct a trial on the charge of murder against George Thomas Holmes of Price's Corners.

"I would remind the witnesses that they will be sworn to tell the truth and held to that truth. I also would remind everyone in this room that this is a serious matter and will be respected as such and ask that you conduct yourself accordingly. Anyone not following those orders will be found in contempt of court." The chief justice glared around the room. Finally he said, "Bring in the prisoner."

Podge was led into the prisoner's dock by Constable Carter. His eyes darted around the room, fearful and bewildered. "Ma," he called out upon seeing his mother. He was dressed in pressed trousers and a fresh shirt that his mother had obviously brought to him. A flash from a camera went off and the hall erupted into yells and jeers.

"String him up!" someone shouted.

"Order!" Chief Justice Brimwell slammed a wooden gavel

onto the table. "There will be order in my court, or I will have everyone not associated with this trial removed!"

The room quieted and the trial began. First Chief O'Brien spoke of the discovery of Mary Ann's bones on Pike's Mountain beneath a spruce tree and how they appeared to have been removed from the original burial site "by the prisoner in the dock as confessed by George Thomas Holmes to myself, Constable Carter, Dr. Hughes, Detective Hardy, and within the hearing of the Price's Corners schoolteacher, Miss Hamilton," and placed under said spruce tree.

"She was lonely," Podge interrupted and was quickly shushed by the police guard.

The crown attorney had the chief point out the location on a map that was then entered as evidence.

Chief O'Brien then went on to describe the whittled carving Vivien had told him about, at which point the chief justice stopped him, saying he'd hear the remainder of the finding of the carving from the girl directly.

Chief O'Brien concluded his testimony by describing the location of Clooey's body in the clearing, found with the "help" of Miss Defiance Vale of Price's Corners. A low murmur and all eyes turned to Dee. She edged closer to her grandmother.

The reporters scribbled frantically. When court let out for a recess, every telephone in Wallen would be in use as they reported back to their newspapers.

Detective Hardy was called next, and he described what he had seen at the site of Clooey's "burial"—piled dirt, obviously turned by a shovel—but admitted that so many members of the public had toured the scene before he got there that it had been difficult to find any evidence that directly related to the crime. He then described his interrogation of Podge, ending with, "I found him to be simple-minded, his intellect that of a five year old, but I believe, in all, a good boy."

Dee felt greatly cheered to hear that—until the chief justice asked for Detective Hardy's last remark to be disregarded by the jury, as it was a speculation on the part of the detective and not fact.

Witnesses came and went, people from the village with exaggerated tales of a murderous Podge roaming the mountain. Dee was outraged.

Just before the lunch hour, Dr. Hughes took the stand.

"I did my post-mortem with the help of my colleague Dr. Britain, from Toronto University. We could not determine the exact cause of death from the bones of Mary Ann Simpson because of their age and the fact there was no tissue remaining."

Dee shivered despite the heat of the room.

"There was, though, an indentation in her skull caused by a blow, but whether or not this was a fatal blow, I cannot tell. It might have been administered to render her unconscious.

There is evidence that a knife had been used on the girl, as the rib bones had nicks in them consistent with a sharp point."

Dr. Hughes looked at his hands, then back up to the jury. "There was also evidence of an unborn child, perhaps three or four months gestation. It is unknown whether the child was male or female."

Dee felt the room stir. Here were the details people had waited in line long hours to hear.

"As we only had the skeleton, there were no internal organs to send away for examination.

"With regard to Constance Eleanor Trewith, we were able to tell a great deal more, as the death was recent. There was a blow to the head also."

A sharp pain shot through Dee's head when she heard this description of Clooey, leaving her feeling ill. She stifled a gasp.

"It is thought to have been the ultimate cause of her death. She also had many knife wounds, including a gash across the throat." Dr. Hughes ran his finger across his own throat, from ear to ear.

The crown attorney interrupted with a question. "Did the wounds appear to have been inflicted by a person experienced with a knife?"

Dr. Hughes stroked his moustache thoughtfully. "I would say, yes, in my experience, this is someone who handles a knife regularly, such as, say, a butcher."

"Or someone who whittles a great deal?"

"That is not my area of expertise, so I cannot say," Dr. Hughes said.

The crown attorney nodded for the doctor to continue.

"As I said, the knife wound, while severe, was not fatal. Perhaps that is why a shovel was used to kill her. Her clothes were blood-soaked and dishevelled. There were signs that she had been interfered with."

A collective gasp filled the room.

"The organs of the girl were extracted and sent to a Toronto university laboratory to be examined. We have the preserved organs with us as evidence."

Two policemen carried in large glass jars filled with yellow liquid in which objects floated—the organs. The room erupted into women's screams of horror. Dee felt sick.

"Order! Order!" The chief justice banged his gavel, to no effect.

A cry sailed above the shouts. "She's fainted!"

Dee turned in her seat to see Clooey's mother being supported by Constable Carter.

"If you could, doctor . . ." The chief justice gestured to the woman. "We'll adjourn for the lunch hour."

Dee and her grandmother sat in the wagon with Mr. Forgetti, Gran on the wagon seat, Dee in the back with a blanket over her knees. While they had been inside the hall, the day had cleared, a watery sun breaking through high cloud. The fresh air felt wonderful after the heat of the hall. Despite that, many people had chosen to stay in the room, reluctant to give up their seats.

Gran saw Podge's mother standing alone on the sidewalk near the hotel, and invited her to join them, but the woman shook her head. "Detective Hardy said he would take me to visit with George during the lunch break."

A few minutes later, the police officer arrived and led her away.

"That's kind of him," Mr. Forgetti said.

"Detective Hardy's a nice man," Dee told him. "He doesn't think Podge killed anyone." She crumbled a slice of bread between her fingers, unable to eat. Images of preserved brains and organs turned over in her mind.

"Don't remember Clooey like that," Gran said, guessing why Dee wasn't hungry. "Remember her smile, those lovely eyes of hers, and the good friend she was to you."

"I am glad I did not go in. It was terrible?" asked Mr. Forgetti.

"Yes, it was terrible," Dee told him.

"A young girl like you. It's not right what you see and hear today," he went on.

A loud laugh brought their heads up to see a group of men swaggering down the street toward them.

"Someone is making money from their still," Gran said. "There won't be anything but trouble from that bunch."

The words were barely out of her mouth when one of the men sauntered over to the wagon.

CHAPTER TWENTY-TWO

The man stopped beside the wagon next to where Gran sat. Short and burly, with light brown hair, he clenched and unclenched his fists. "Here's that old lady who's the witch. Sitting with that foreigner," he shouted back to his friends. He faced Mr. Forgetti. "We fought a lot of your kind overseas."

"I did not fight you. I stayed here and worked in the mill to make cloth and blankets for the Canadian soldiers and worked on my farm to feed people," Mr. Forgetti said.

The man swayed on his feet. "Your lot would just as soon slit a person's throat as look at them. If they hadn't arrested that retarded man for the murders, you would have been my next choice." He peered into the back of the wagon. "And it's that girl. Apple doesn't fall far from the tree, does it? Can you tell me my future, girl?"

He reached into the wagon as if to grab Dee, but she crawled away from him.

Mr. Forgetti stood up. "You leave that girl alone." He made to climb down from the wagon, but Gran held up a hand to stop him.

"We don't want any trouble. It's a hard time for everyone. I would ask that you please leave," she said to the men.

"So you know there's going to be trouble? I guess you do know things before they happen." The man slammed the side of the wagon with the flat of his hand. Dee jumped. "But then again, maybe it's you who killed those girls. You and that idiot working together. Maybe that's why you can't tell anyone who did it, because it's you!"

Muttering their agreement, the other men came forward and grouped behind the first. Dee didn't know them, though she thought they were workers from the mill. A few had on their military greatcoats. So they weren't too long returned from the war, she figured. They all were looking for a fight. People drifted over to see what was going on, and before long, a large crowd enclosed the wagon. Dee looked around. Where was Constable Carter when you wanted him?

"Leave them alone," a man's voice rang out.

Ray Price pushed between the men and shoved two of the closest away from the wagon.

"You're with them?" The first man asked.

"I'm with no one. There are women here and police every-where. You want to go to jail? Pay a fine? You got the money

to do that then go ahead. Go ahead and fight him—and me."
Ray stood in front of the wagon, arms crossed.

With a great deal of grumbling, the men slowly turned
away.

"Thank you," Mr. Forgetti said.

Ray Price ignored Mr. Forgetti and spoke directly to Dee's
grandmother. "So we're even now. You helped my wife and I
helped you."

"Yes," Gran said.

Satisfied, Ray nodded and left.

Gradually, the crowd broke up, anxious to get back to the
town hall. Glancing at her grandmother, Dee was surprised to
see the woman looked old, thin, and pale. She had never, Dee
realized, given any thought to the toll the trial was taking on her
gran. As they returned to the town hall, Dee took her grandmother's arm, this time being comforter rather than comforted.

As before, Podge was escorted to the prisoner's dock, looking a little happier after his visit with his mother. He saw Dee
and waved to her. She waved back and noticed a newspaper
man bend to his notebook. She knew he was writing about
her. She didn't care what they said. She was Podge's friend and
would always be Podge's friend.

Chief Justice Brimwell repeated the court procedure, and
the trial continued.

Dr. Hughes was reminded that he was still under oath as
he took the witness stand.

"Do you believe the man George Thomas Holmes capable of these horrendous crimes?"

The hall quieted. Dee heard an automobile horn outside, a bird call, and a splatter of freezing rain against one of the arched windows—the weather must have turned yet again, typical of fall, Dee thought inconsequentially.

Dr. Hughes stroked his moustache over and over, then let his hand drop to his lap. "It is difficult to know what the mentally infirm are capable of. We have no idea of their thought processes. Could he have murdered these two girls? I can give you only my opinion, and please remember I am not a doctor who deals with diseases of the mind, but yes, I believe it's possible he harmed those girls, and I also believe that Mr. Holmes might not even be aware of his actions. He has a man's urges and strengths but the mind of a child. I believe Mr. Holmes is a danger to himself and to society at large and should be put away where he cannot harm anyone."

Podge's mother, distraught, cried out, "No!"

Frightened, Podge began to wail. He tried to leave the dock, but the two policemen pushed him back.

When he'd settled back down, Vivien was called to testify. She told of finding the carved bird near the spot where the bones had been and then pointed to Dee. "She took the carving from me and told me to not tell anyone."

Dee felt herself grow hot. She'd never said that last bit, she was sure.

Dee's name was called. Legs shaking so much she had barely been able to walk, she sat down in the witness chair, for the first time facing the people crowded into the hall. She put her hand on the Bible and swore the oath, that before God she would tell the truth. Eagerly she searched the faces, saw Billy, and then found Clarence standing alone near the back. Just his being there made her feel a bit better.

Reluctantly, Dee admitted taking the carving from Vivien, adding that she had never said to not tell anyone. "Lots of people have Podge's carvings," she said. "He gives them away as gifts, and any one of them could have dropped a whittled animal on the mountain." So she hadn't given the carved bird much thought after that. She answered more questions about Clooey and Mary Ann, answers she'd already given Chief O'Brien.

"And you heard the defendant say that he moved Miss Simpson's body underneath *your* tree?"

"Yes," Dee admitted miserably. "But I think he found her dead and . . ."

"That will be all." The crown attorney cut her off.

Now it was the defence lawyer's turn. "Miss Vale, how did you *know* where to find Constance's body? Did anyone suggest where she might be found? Say, your grandmother?"

Dee felt stunned. Was the lawyer going to blame her grandmother? It was his job to protect Podge, but to involve Gran to do so was preposterous.

"No. No one told me where to look. Clooey—Constance—

and I played in that clearing when we were younger. I thought if she was hurt and couldn't get off the mountain, she would go there and wait. She knew I'd come and find her. That's why I went there, looking for her hat, or her coat, anything that showed she'd been there. It was a place to start looking. I stumbled on her grave," she finished in a whisper.

"That is all," the lawyer said.

As Dee made her way back to her seat, she noticed many of the men pull out handkerchiefs to mop their faces and the ladies fanning themselves. The temperature in the hall was rising. With a shock, she realized one of the women was Mrs. Hughes. The doctor's wife was huddled in a chair near the back corner of the room, a large hat shadowing her face. She raised it now and stared directly at Dee. Never had Dee seen anyone so pale. They locked eyes, and Dee thought she saw sympathy in the woman's glance, and again, the terror. With difficulty, Dee tore her gaze away and sat down, facing the front of the hall. She wondered if Dr. Hughes knew his wife was there. But she soon forgot Mrs. Hughes, for she heard her grandmother's name called.

A buzz went around the room as Gran made her way to the stand, everyone eager to hear her testimony. Detective Hardy slipped into her grandmother's empty seat beside Dee.

"I am sorry," he murmured.

For what? Dee wondered.

The crown attorney was asking Gran about Mary Ann.

"I've been a midwife all my life," Gran replied. "I can tell if a woman is in the family way, often before she knows herself." She then went on to say that she wasn't sure if even Mary Ann knew she was expecting, and that she thought Mary Ann had been taken advantage of because of her young age. Dee knew that Mr. Simpson would take that statement as the kindness it was meant to be.

After half an hour of questions, the crown attorney sat down, and the defence lawyer stood up. He looked at his notes for a few minutes, then said, "I understand you are not a churchgoing woman, so I would ask that you please verify that you understand you are under oath to tell the truth."

"I have no quarrel with God," Gran said. "I made the oath to tell the truth with Him, not a building."

"Keep that oath in mind when I will ask you outright, Madam, if you had anything to do with the murder of these girls."

"I did not."

"I've been told you have special—um—abilities, a certain foreknowledge of events. Is this true?"

"Yes, if you can call using common sense a special ability," Gran said. "But it is true that I have an extra sensitivity to some things that others do not."

Dee felt the crowd behind her lean forward, everyone perched on the edge of their chairs, their interest in the woman in the witness stand unwavering.

Dee could see Gran brace herself and realized that Gran
knew what question was coming next.

The lawyer shuffled some papers. "I understand you have a
daughter of your own, Mrs. Vale."

"I do," Gran said.

"And she is the mother of your granddaughter, Defiance,
who sits here today."

"She is." Dee's grandmother sat perfectly still, her face
expressionless.

"I will ask you then, Mrs. Vale, if you know the whereabouts of your daughter?"

"I do."

Dee felt the air leave her lungs.

"And she is not singing with a travelling show as you have
told people, is she?" the lawyer thundered. He turned and faced
the crowd, eyebrows raised. "Will you tell the jury where your
daughter is at this very moment and why?"

There was a long moment of silence, then Dee's grandmother turned slightly and spoke directly to Dee. "I would not
have you learn of your mother this way, but I am under oath
and must tell the truth. I ask that you forgive me."

Dee smelled it first; decay, the stink of rotting flesh. Gag-
ging, she saw the black pillar form behind the chief justice,
towering from floor to ceiling. She felt its heat.

"What?" Detective Hardy shook her arm. "What do you
see?"

"Evil," Dee breathed.

The detective covered one of Dee's hands with his own. "Hold on. I'm going to get you out of here."

"No," Dee pulled back.

Gran had turned back to the lawyer. "This is a dreadful thing that you are doing."

The shadow gathered substance, countless faces, mouths gaping open in silent screams, churning in the middle. Dee tightened her grip on Detective Hardy's hand, her knuckles turning white.

Her grandmother drew herself up. "She is in an insane asylum outside Hamilton."

Dee struggled for breath. She heard Vivien's gasp, heard the whispers behind her.

"And what was the cause of her insanity?" The defence lawyer raised his voice to be heard over the shocked murmurs in the town hall.

Dee fought the light-headedness that threatened to pull her into a faint. She needed to know.

"Fifteen years ago," her grandmother said, "my daughter was attacked and left for dead. I found her, up the mountain, bleeding. I carried her home and cared for her until the babe, my granddaughter, was born. But my daughter's mind was broken by the horror she'd endured. For her sake and for the sake of the baby, the stigma that child would have to live under, I put my daughter into the insane asylum and told people that she had gone away."

"Do you think it was the same man as harmed these girls?"

"I don't know." Gran seemed to shrink in her chair, weary now that the truth she had carried for so long was out. "It was the same type of attack. My daughter had been stabbed, but she lived. To this day she is unable to tell me or anyone else what happened to her up on the mountain. I visit her once a month, but she does not know who I am. There is nothing further I can tell you."

The defence lawyer turned to the jury. "But George Thomas Holmes was merely eleven years old at that time. Men of the jury, I put it to you that a child of eleven years could not have carried out this heinous crime."

"You did this!" Dee cried. She pushed Detective Hardy away from her. "You did this. You found out where my mother was." The black spread up the walls of the hall and across the floor, flowing beneath the chairs of the chief justice and his secretaries.

Podge began to scream, pointing at it, but no one else could see it, except Dee.

"I thought you were a friend, a good man." She began to weep.

"It was the only way I could cast doubt that George had done these murders," Detective Hardy told her gently. "I needed to prove he could be innocent."

CHAPTER TWENTY-THREE

"I am sorry. I was wrong to have kept this secret about your mother from you."

Dee had never heard her grandmother, this woman who was always sure of herself, sound so uncertain. But she didn't care. She was too full of hurt and anger. All this time, she had thought that she, Dee, wasn't good enough to bring her mother home. "I had a right to know about my mother. And if you had said something back then, maybe Clooey wouldn't have died!" Dee cried.

"I know that now. I did what I thought was best at the time," Gran said.

Mr. Forgetti clicked to the horses to speed them up. "That's all a person can do," he said, distraught at the way the trial had ended and at Dee's anger.

Night had fallen, and the icy rain had turned to snow. Mud splashed up from the horses' hooves to wet the three of them crowded together on the wagon seat. Miserable and cold, Dee huddled under a blanket.

"What about the seashell? You said Mama sent it."

"No," Gran told her. "You found it one day and made up that story that your mother had sent it. It was given to me by your grandfather many, many years ago. Shortly after we were married, he had to go away on business for Mr. Richmond, to look over some cotton. He was at the ocean and he brought that back for me. When you first noticed the shell, well, you were so little. You read the note and thought it was from your Mama and you were so pleased. I decided, what was the harm . . ."

The harm?

"But it was a lie; it wasn't true," Dee said. Now even that, the comfort of the shell, was gone from her.

"And Detective Hardy," Dee went on. "He dug around in our lives. He ruined everything."

"He was just doing his job. He put doubt in peoples' minds that George had something to do with the murders," Gran said.

After Gran's disclosure, the chief justice had adjourned the trial pending further investigation.

"I'll never be able to face people in Price's Corners ever again. They already think we're crazy, and this just proves it," Dee said.

"Your mama is not crazy," Gran said sternly. "Her mind shut down after the attack to protect her. It was too terrible for her to think about."

The wagon rattled over ruts as Mr. Forgetti pulled to the side of the road to let an automobile pass.

Dee slumped against the wooden seatback, feeling bruised all over. In her heart, she knew it wasn't her grandmother or Detective Hardy who had destroyed her life. It was evil. Detective Hardy had just done his job, studying the village, turning the lives of everyone over as if they were rocks, to find what secrets lay beneath. An unsavoury business his was, not for everyone, and in his own way, Dee realized, he was as *special* as she and Gran.

And then she realized something else. "I'm the daughter of a murderer," she blurted out.

"There is nothing bad in you," Gran told her.

"How do you know that? How do you know I don't have some evil in me, too?" Dee asked. Her heart beat unevenly.

They had come into Price's Corners and were passing the church and graveyard. She stared at the schoolhouse, at Simpsons' Mercantile, at the church, and the police house. They seemed foreign to her, changed, even though they were solidly made of stone and wood. It was she who was different.

Outside town, the night closed in around them. Through the light rain she could just make out the black shadow of Pike's Mountain. All those times she'd played up there—had her foot ever fell in the very spot that her mother had lain, hurt and bleeding? She'd lost her mountain forever.

When they reached the house, Dee and Gran got down from the wagon and saw Mr. Forgetti off. Then Dee turned to her grandmother. "I'm just going to sit outside here on the step," she said. "I need to be by myself. I need to think."

Her grandmother nodded and took her shawl from her shoulders and wrapped it around Dee. "Don't get too cold," she said.

Dee settled onto the top step, her back against the door. She pulled Gran's shawl over her head to keep the snow from her hair. She'd told Gran she needed to think, but now that she was alone, she couldn't grasp a single thought, so she just sat, spent from the day's events. From the fenced pen at the side of the house she heard the soft cluck of the chickens and Trojan snorting in his sleep. The moon broke through the cloud and washed the road in white light before slipping behind the cloud again and plunging the world back into darkness. But the momentary light had been enough for Dee to see the glistening of wet metal beneath the trees. She stood up and slowly walked down the porch steps and into the road and, after a moment, moved closer to the ditch. From here, she could see the outline of an automobile that had been driven into the trees. She wanted to move closer, see whose motor vehicle it was, but quickly realized it didn't matter. Whoever had been in the automobile had gone up the mountain. She would find him there.

She waited for a few minutes, listening, but there was no

sound other than that of the rushing stream. It was foolhardy going up the mountain at night, alone, but what if someone, another girl, was in danger? She couldn't save Clooey, but she might be able to help this time.

She began to climb, avoiding the main path. Her feet slid on wet leaves and mud, tiring her. After half an hour, she stopped to catch her breath. She'd made it this far, but now what? She'd not seen anyone and didn't know which way to go. From behind a wide maple, she caught a glimpse of a silver shimmer. She watched it take a girl's form.

"Clooey!" Dee cried.

The haunt wavered, faded, and then became stronger. Dee caught the motion of one arm, signalling her to follow.

Desperate to keep up with the spirit, Dee pushed through thickets, uncaring as thorns tore at her coat sleeves and hands. Then, as unexpectedly as she had appeared, Clooey vanished. Dee felt a stab of pain to lose her friend again, but saw that Clooey's haunt had led her to the clearing where her grave had been.

Dee waited until the moon came out again and showed that the field was empty before she stepped out from the woods. Clooey's spirit had led her here, so there had to be something to be found, something that she had missed, a clue to the identity of the killer.

Dead stalks of grass and weeds soaked the hem of her skirt as she picked her way through the clearing. Nothing stirred.

No night creatures called or moved through the trees. She became acutely aware of the strangeness of the night, the air of waiting. Shivering, she looked around the field and saw it was ringed by silver shimmers, spirits.

"Clooey, I don't know what you mean," Dee whispered, well aware that the owner of the automobile could be nearby.

She felt movement behind her and twisted around so fast she lost her balance and nearly fell.

"What are you doing up here?" Clarence asked. "It's dangerous. Can't you feel it?" He looked around at the night, head bare, hair glowing golden.

"There's a motor vehicle at the bottom of the mountain," Dee told him. "I wanted to know who was here, and, well, Clooey—her spirit—brought me here." Better just to let him know everything. "Clarence, I can see people's spirits after they've died and I have *feelings*, hunches, whatever you want to call them. I know and see things other people don't. I'm different," she repeated.

"I'm different, too," Clarence said calmly. "I think I'm like you."

"You are?" Dee was so grateful he understood.

"Dee, he's coming," Clarence said urgently.

"Who?" Dee asked eagerly.

"I can't . . ." Clarence stopped and rubbed his forehead. "He killed them."

"Clooey and Mary Ann?"

"Yes, and the—the others," he said. "There was at least one other girl. Probably more. In France. During the war. He, of all people, to do such a terrible thing. I wouldn't have believed it if I hadn't seen it with my own eyes." Clarence gripped his head in anguish. "I can't remember who! I saw him at the trial, but I can't remember."

"Clarence," Dee said. "You have to remember. Please!"

"That's the problem, Dee. I'm forgetting all the time. I'd forgotten you, until I saw you here now. I'm losing—me." He shook his head, then stopped, alert. "You have to leave right now. You're in danger!"

"I can't," Dee said. "He attacked my mother, Clarence. Like all the others, and he left her here on the mountain, except she didn't die, she's still alive."

"That doesn't matter; you need to go."

"I have to find out who he is. Don't you see, Clarence? He's my father. The murderer is my father. I exist because he attacked my mother," she sobbed. "I thought maybe if I saw him up here, I could stop him from hurting anyone else. He's evil and he's my father."

Clarence looked out over the clearing, then back at Dee. "There is no evil in you. I would know. I've seen evil up close."

"Clooey brought me here for a reason, Clarence. I think I need to go to her grave."

"Quickly, then, there's not much time," Clarence said.

They struck out across the field toward the snow-covered mound of earth.

"There's been a man here many times," Clarence said. "He walks around, and then he hides and waits."

"Is he small with a beard?" Dee asked.

Clarence nodded.

"That would be Detective Hardy. He says that killers often return to the place they committed their crimes, so he must have been watching in case this man did, too."

As they neared the spot, Dee saw that there were no fresh footsteps in the newly fallen snow. "He's not been here yet tonight," she said.

She stared at the shallow grave, breathing hard. "I have to get right into it to *feel* what Clooey felt. I have to *feel* her death," she said.

"I don't think . . ." Clarence began.

But Dee stepped down into the narrow grave. Immediately, her head spun with pain and fear. She pushed past it, looking for something, anything to help her discover who had murdered Clooey.

"She wasn't killed here," Dee said. "I mean, Clooey *was* killed here, but she wasn't supposed to be. He thought she was dead and brought her here to bury her, but she was still alive. That's why he had to hit her with the shovel. To kill her.

But . . ." she shook her head, frustrated. "I don't know where he had her first. I wonder . . . I'll have to get right in. I have to lie where Clooey lay, where she died."

"No!" Clarence protested. "You could get pulled into her death. You could die yourself."

"It's the only way. The ground, it holds the last bit of Clooey. She wasn't dead when he buried her the first time, so her energy will have seeped into the dirt. I'll be able to be with her at the moment of her death. I'll know who did it."

Dee shuddered and closed her eyes. *It's the only way,* she told herself as she stepped in and stretched out in the grave.

Terror. It nearly undid Dee. Her first instinct was to flee the grave, flee the mountain itself and be done with it. She fought the impulse and felt herself slip into darkness. But no, that would not do either. This was not her death! She needed to hold onto her own self: think of Cissy, school, her plans to be a nurse, and her grandmother, mostly her grandmother. Abruptly, she could *see* Clooey's memories.

The dance. Carved pumpkins. Apples floating in kettles of water. Fiddle music. Laughter. Excitement. Going to see the fortune teller. It's only Miss Hamilton. Disappointment. Too hot. Need to get some air. Stepping outside the schoolhouse. The door shutting. Noise fading. Walking down the steps to the swings at the side of the play yard. Sitting on a wooden seat and gently swinging to and fro. The moon full above. No one else here. Hands rough about her waist.

A cloth over the mouth. Can't breathe. Strange smell. Darkness.

Feel sick. Drowsy. Wood panelling on the walls. Large wood cabinet in the corner. Bottles on the shelves. Hard table beneath. Try to get up, but can't move. Tied down. That smell. Familiar.

Dee groaned in the grave.

A brown-sleeved arm, rough fabric (wool?), a hand coming toward her face. Pushing her hair from her cheek. A whisper, "So pretty. So pretty. But why did you leave the dance?" A knife gently cutting through her Sunday dress, cutting through her skin. "If you had only stayed at the party. I wouldn't have found you." A face above, can't see, lost in shadows. Who are you? The smell stronger now. So familiar.

Dee screamed and scrambled out of the trench, sobbing and retching.

"I know who it is! I know who it is! He's going to kill another girl. I have to get to town and find Detective Hardy. Stay here. Stop him."

"Who?" Clarence yelled after her.

CHAPTER TWENTY-FOUR

Dee ran blindly through the black night, tears flooding her eyes. She could feel the mountain's bulk above her, but she couldn't see it or the trees in front of her. She wiped a sleeve across her face but the tears immediately welled up again. The horrible things he'd done to Clooey, cutting her, hurting her.

She ran headfirst into a tree trunk. Stunned, she stopped to steady herself against a boulder. As much as she didn't want to, she'd have to slow down. One misstep and she could twist or break an ankle and then she'd be of no use to anyone. Carefully, she picked her way down the path.

She knew now why she hadn't *seen* the threat over Clooey. The killer hadn't planned her abduction. Clooey just happened to be in the wrong place, and the killer had taken advantage of the opportunity. In the narrow grave, Dee had not only relived Clooey's memories; the killer had left part of himself, too. He did not know that the blood-bond between him and Dee allowed her to *feel* him, to feel the struggle within him:

not wanting to take Clooey, not liking the spontaneity of it, but the driving desire of evil inside him that had made him act. She'd also *felt* his surprise and subsequent enjoyment of killing Clooey—twice. What she had not felt from him was remorse, guilt, shame, or responsibility for taking Clooey's life. He also had not known that their shared blood would let her see who his next victim was. Vivien. The shadow on Vivien's face—why had she not realized it before?

Dee shied away from thinking of the killer. In her heightened state of emotion, she feared she'd give herself away to him, especially—and she hated the very thought—with the biological bond between them. She focused instead on getting down the mountain safely.

A steady wind scattered the clouds across the sky, letting moonlight through. And then, almost at the bottom of the mountain, Dee saw another light, a flickering orange-yellow light in the distance. Fire! And it was coming from the direction of her house!

She put on a burst of speed, the wood bridge ringing beneath her hard-soled boots. She didn't care who heard her now. Her house was on fire, and Gran was inside!

As she ran up the road, she saw a second automobile parked in the ditch but she gave it no thought as she ran past. In front of her house, Dee stopped, horrified by the smoke billowing into the dark sky from the windows and open front door.

"Gran!" Dee screamed above the crackle of the dancing fire.

Coughing, she ran up the porch steps, but as she was about to step over the threshold, there was a *boom* and glass exploded around her. Her grandmother's bedroom window. Then came another explosion: of suspicion, hostility, and hate. It was here. The evil was inside. Dee tried again to go in the door, but the smoke rose, forming a familiar black pillar that blocked her path. She retched at the stench, helpless to move.

A shove from behind sent her sprawling into the house, right through the pillar. It fell apart around her and swirled away into the night.

"Sorry," a woman's choked voice said from behind her. "I had to—you were standing—and . . ." A light touch on Dee's arm. "Keep down, below the smoke. We'll save her."

Crawling on all fours, Dee followed the woman into the kitchen. She wanted to shout for her grandmother, but the heat of the fire stole her breath away, leaving none for words. A roof beam crashed down onto the table near the window, showering embers over them. Dee covered her head with both hands.

"Here!" The woman's voice, faint over the roar of the flames, drew Dee farther into the room.

She put out her hand, feeling along the floor, and found an arm, warm but unmoving. Dee crept closer and ran her hand higher up to a shoulder, a head, and below, a sticky pool. Blood.

"No! No!" Dee screamed and pawed at her grandmother's body.

"Grab her legs. We have to pull her out before the house collapses."

Breathing heavily, they slowly dragged Dee's grandmother to the front door, an endless journey, and down the steps, where they laid her on the front path out of harm's way.

The woman collapsed beside her, coughing.

Dee carefully cradled her grandmother's head in her lap. There was no sign of life. "Please, Gran. Oh please. Don't leave me," she cried.

Finally, Gran rolled her head from side to side, coughed and opened her eyes to see Dee's face. A trembling, blistered hand gently stroked Dee's cheek. "Not my time," Gran whispered.

Dee hugged her grandmother and sat back on her heels, laughing and crying at the same time. If anyone would *know* it was their time to die, it would be Gran. A roar brought their eyes to the burning house in time to see the roof collapse, sparks like shooting stars rising into the night sky.

She finally looked at the woman who had helped her, and in the flames' dancing light saw it was Mrs. Hughes.

"You knew," Dee said.

Mrs. Hughes looked down at her own soot-covered hands. "Yes. But I was too weak, too powerless to stop him. Until I saw you." She raised her eyes to Dee. "It was you who made me speak up. You live up to your name, Defiance. It was you who gave me strength."

"I'm his daughter," Dee said.

"By blood, but not by deed," Mrs. Hughes told her.

Vivien's mother came running through the side field to where they sat. "I've sent the boys for help. Vivien's missing! I can't find her anywhere." She sank to her knees beside Dee and Mrs. Hughes. "He's got her. That murderer has her." She buried her head in her hands and wept.

Esther tugged on Dee's sleeve. Dee hadn't even seen the younger girl arrive. "Dr. Hughes brought Vivien back from the trial in his automobile," Esther said. Her eyes were wide with shock. "Mama was having a sleep so she didn't see. He parked across from your house." She pointed to where the doctor's motor vehicle was parked among the trees. "Vivien was sleeping, so he put her over his shoulder. He had a shovel with him. Your gran came out and tried to stop him. He dropped Vivien right in the road and he hit your gran on the head with the shovel and dragged her back into the house! I wanted to help Vivien, but I was scared." Esther began to cry. "I was afraid he'd hurt me, too. So I hid."

"Hush." Mrs. Hughes put her arm around Esther. "I was scared, too."

"After he left I woke Mama and we saw the flames."

Mrs. Hughes gestured toward the cars farther up the road, nearer the mountain. "I came with Detective Hardy. I told the detective. I finally told someone. He's gone up the mountain after him."

Dee felt torn inside. She didn't know what to do. She wanted to help Vivien but didn't want to leave Gran.

"Defiance," Gran gasped. "Go. Catch up to the others. Stop him. You need to do this."

"I'll send help to follow as soon as it arrives," Mrs. Hughes promised.

Dee's mind cleared, all uncertainty gone. Already she could hear the shouts of her neighbours coming down the road. They would help Gran, though the house was beyond saving. But now, the monster had to be stopped; the pain and sorrow he caused had to end. And her gran had said that she, Dee, needed to do it; Gran, who *knew*. She bent down and gave her grandmother a swift kiss on the cheek.

"Take care, Defiance," Gran whispered.

Dee ran back over the bridge and up the path. He'd be carrying Vivien, so hopefully that would slow him down. She knew exactly where he was going: to the clearing.

The wet snow had finally stopped, but the damp lingered, rising from the ground like white steam to wrap around weeds and tree trunks, burrow into bushes, and hide the path. Dee stopped climbing, enveloped by the dense fog, afraid she was running in circles. She, who knew the mountain, was lost.

A silver shimmer appeared in front of her and then a second one a few steps ahead, followed by a third. The air hissed around Dee, and the night came alive as the haunts gathered energy, disturbed by the wickedness that had gone up the mountain before her.

Dee moved forward confidently in the midst of the spirits, who showed her the way, hoping to come across Detective Hardy and Chief O'Brien. If not, well, Clarence would be in the clearing, where she'd left him. But how could a mere girl and a damaged soldier stop a determined killer?

The fog thinned out and cleared completely as she climbed higher. Dee began to recognize landmarks—a stump shaped like a hunched man, an overhanging branch from an oak— and then she was in the trees before the clearing.

She stepped cautiously now, but despite her care, a twig snapped sharply beneath her boot. Dee froze. She stood still a long moment, listening. Hearing nothing, she stooped beneath the low-hanging vines and stepped into the clearing. As she did, an arm came around her neck and pulled her down. A hand covered her mouth. Dee fought hard, kicking and scratching.

"Quiet," a voice breathed in her ear. "It's Detective Hardy and Chief O'Brien."

Dee sagged with relief as the hand fell from her mouth. She crept back into the trees and crouched down. They waited quietly for a few minutes, then Detective Hardy said, "I think he's here."

Moonlight on the newly fallen snow lit the clearing like

day. A shadowy figure staggered into view, a woman hung limply over one shoulder. Dee feared the way the girl's head lolled so freely. Had they gotten to Vivien in time?

"Clarence, Vivien's brother, is out there somewhere. We need to help him rescue her," Dee whispered.

She started to get to her feet, but Detective Hardy held her down.

"Wait," he said. "I need to see him dig the grave in order to convict him."

"But what if Vivien isn't dead yet?" Dee whispered.

"You have to let me do this my way," Detective Hardy insisted.

"No! He's killed my friends and other girls. He made my mother go mad. I won't let him hurt anyone ever again." She yanked her arm out of the detective's grip and dashed into the clearing.

"Let her go! Let Vivien go, Dr. Hughes!" she screamed.

The shadowy figure turned toward her, abruptly dropped his bundle in a heap on the ground, and began to run. Dee could hear him crashing through the trees.

She ran over to Vivien and fell beside the girl. Seconds later, Detective Hardy and Chief O'Brien knelt down next to her. The chief placed a hand on the side of Vivien's neck. "She's still alive." He pulled up her eyelids. "Drugged."

"He wanted to kill her with a shovel. He enjoyed killing Clooey that way. I *felt* it," Dee sobbed.

"Dee, you stay with Vivien and Chief O'Brien," Detective Hardy ordered. He fished out a gun from under his topcoat.

"No, I'm coming with you," Dee said. "He's headed to the falls. I know the way. I can show you." She started through the trees. Where, she wondered, was Clarence? Following Dr. Hughes?

In and out of the tree trunks Dee wove, Detective Hardy behind her, as they followed the killer's wild flight.

Eventually, another noise drowned the sound of breaking branches: the rumble of the waterfall. They burst out from behind a tree to see dark water tumble over the cliff. Over its roar, Dee heard a terrified scream and saw Dr. Hughes, face contorted by terror, slowly stepping backwards until he teetered on the edge of the gorge. There was nowhere left for him to go.

"Get away!" he shrieked. "Leave me alone."

He stood as silver light advanced on him, the spirits of all the girls he'd killed steadily forcing him to the cliff edge, to his death. So many, Dee thought, her mind reeling. He had killed so many!

And then she saw, in the middle of them, glowing bright silver—Clarence. Everything receded from Dee's mind—the screams of the terrified killer, the thunder of water; her vision narrowed until there was only the young man in his army uniform. How had she not *seen*? Because, she scolded herself, you didn't want to.

"What is it? What is going on? What do you *see*?" Detective Hardy shook her arm.

"It's all the girls he's murdered. Their spirits." Dee turned to the detective. "They've come for him. They are going to make him fall over the cliff to his death."

Dr. Hughes pushed and punched wildly at the air, trying to break through the wall of haunts, but the only way left open to him was over the cliff, into the fall's whirlpool.

"Can you stop them?" Detective Hardy asked.

Dee pointed to the doctor. "He's being punished by the girls he killed. Is this not justice?"

Detective Hardy turned her around to face him. "No, it isn't. Not in a civilized society. He needs to be tried for his crimes in a court of law. He needs to face the families he hurt. This way is too easy for him."

While he spoke, Dee saw that a group of men had gathered behind the detective: Constable Carter, Billy and his father, Ray Price, Mr. Richmond, and Mr. Simpson among them, faces grim.

The detective was right. These men needed to see Dr. Hughes given a trial, needed to hear him condemned by his peers, by men who believed in good. She saw that now.

Dee nodded. "I'll try to talk to them. They just want peace; they want it over, want to rest."

She pushed through the spirits, passing Mary Ann and Clooey, coming to stand beside Clarence. "Vivien?" he asked.

"She's alive," Dee told him. Her heart broke when she looked into his kind face, veiled now with the telltale grey shimmer of death. But she'd have to deal with that sadness later.

She turned to the terrified man in front of her. "Dr. Hughes."

He reached out his hands toward her, pleading, "Help me! What is happening? I can feel them, but I can't see them."

"These are the ghosts of the girls you murdered. They have come for you," Dee said.

"Stop them," Dr. Hughes pleaded. "*You* can tell them to go away."

"Why would I?" Dee said. "You're a doctor. You're supposed to save people. People trusted you, believed in you. But you took their lives away. Maybe it's a sickness, one even a doctor can't cure. But you have to be stopped."

"Help me, Dee," he cried. "I'm your father! I would never hurt you. Don't let them kill me."

"But you did hurt me! My friends . . ." Dee choked back a sob.

"You're my daughter. You're part of me!" Dr. Hughes cried. "It's because of me that you want to be a nurse."

"No!" Dee shouted, fury giving her a voice. "There is no part of you in me. If there were, I would let these spirits have their way. I would let them kill you. But I won't. I will save you from them because I don't want your death on my hands."

She turned to the shimmering circle. "We will take him to trial, and he will confess and be found guilty and will hang for his crimes," she said gently. "I am asking you to let us honour you this way, to let people know what happened to you, to celebrate your life. And we will let them know what kind of a monster ended it." She pointed to Dr. Hughes.

"Who is she talking to?" she heard Chief O'Brien ask the detective.

"I believe she speaks to the shades of the murdered girls," Detective Hardy said.

"It's time for you all to pass over now. It is done. Thank you." Dee nodded to Detective Hardy.

He and Chief O'Brien pulled Dr. Hughes away from the cliff edge and handed him over to Constable Carter. The men parted as the constable and Ray Price pushed the doctor ahead of them to take him down the mountain. The others followed silently, except Mr. Richmond and Mr. Simpson, who stayed.

"Is my daughter here?" Mr. Richmond asked. "My Elizabeth?"

Dee turned to him. "Yes. She's here. She's standing beside me. She says she's sorry you've suffered so much grief, but she wants you to know that she's content at last and that she loves you. She's going now to join her mother."

"Give my love to them both," Mr. Richmond said gruffly.

"And mine to Mary Ann. Tell her, her mother and me, we

think about her and miss her every day," Mr. Simpson said.

"She thinks about you, too," Dee said. She smiled at her long-dead friend, holding a baby in her arms. "She says to tell her mother that she's at peace and is with her baby boy."

She watched for a moment as both girls turned and walked toward the cliff edge. A grieving wind whispered through the trees, speaking of heartbreak and loss, of peace and love. It pulled apart the silver shimmering veils and drew them high into the air, where they sparkled, then winked out of sight.

"They've passed over now," Dee said. "They're finished with our world."

The men nodded their thanks and left, leaving Dee alone with Detective Hardy.

There were just two spirits remaining.

Heart heavy, Dee turned to Clooey. "I'm so sorry I couldn't save you," she said.

"It's not your fault," Clooey told her. "Go and be a nurse, see the ocean and the mountains." Clooey smiled. "Live your life, for me."

"I love you," Dee mouthed the words as Clooey faded away. There would be many sorrow-filled nights missing her friend.

"There's just one more I need to speak to," Dee said.

Detective Hardy nodded but didn't move.

"It's private," Dee told him.

"Oh. Yes. Of course." Detective Hardy walked to the edge of the cliff and watched the water rush over the falls.

Dee turned to Clarence. "I didn't know you were a ghost. I don't know why I couldn't *see* that."

"I didn't know myself until tonight," Clarence told her. "I mean, I think I did, the way I was forgetting everything. I felt like I was fading away, but I didn't want to believe I was dead. It wasn't the war that killed me. It was him. That doctor. There was a hospital set up in a village in France just behind the front lines. I got some shrapnel in my leg, so I was convalescing there. A couple of girls went missing from the village, but it was wartime." He shrugged. "Then one night, I went out to the latrine, and I saw him pulling a girl into the woods. It didn't sit right with me, so I followed. I stumbled on him stabbing her in the chest. I yelled and thought to save her, but he turned on me. With my leg hurt, I couldn't run and he killed me. Somehow I found my way back, to here, to Vivien and my family, and to him, that killer."

"You came back to save Vivien," Dee said.

Clarence held his arms out to Dee then let them drop, knowing he wasn't able to touch her.

"I guess it's done now. I'm still there, Dee, in those woods in France, and no one knows where my body lies."

"I know," Dee said.

"I'm too young to be dead, Dee," Clarence cried. "I want to be alive, and I want to be with you. I love you, Dee."

Dee leaned toward him and whispered, "I love you, Clarence. You're a good man, and I wish you could stay. But you have to pass over. You go now, and get some rest. You must be so tired."

"I guess I am that," Clarence agreed.

The wind picked up again, and slowly the silver veil whirled about him and broke apart. "Tell Ma and the children I love them."

"I will," Dee promised.

"I'll miss you and your mountain."

"I'll miss you, too," she whispered.

And then she heard, floating on the wind, so gentle it was merely a sigh, the name of a village in France.

CHAPTER TWENTY-FIVE

Dee sat on the train's hard seat beside her grandmother. December snow fell thickly, coating the branches of the bushes that lined the rails. Small white eddies danced away from the train's wheels, moving across the fields. The spicy scent of the pine boughs she'd cut and tied together with red ribbon filled the car. They were for her mother for Christmas. She and Gran were on their way to the Woodford Insane Asylum near Hamilton.

"You don't have to go in," Gran suddenly said.

"Yes, I do," Dee replied. She needed to see her mama. "I'll be fine, Gran."

She sat back and watched the world fly past the steam-streaked window. It had been a busy few weeks since Dr. Hughes had been arrested for murder. He sat now in the Wallen jail awaiting trial.

"Gran, how long do you think Mrs. Hughes knew what her husband was? She always seemed like—" Dee searched for a word to describe the woman, "—like a wisp of smoke that could be easily blown away. At the funeral lunch for Mary Ann, she looked right at me, and I had the feeling she knew who I was. I mean, who I *really* was."

"I expect she's known for some time but didn't want to believe it of him. Perhaps that's why she was so reclusive," Gran said. "It was a way to ignore her knowledge and keep her husband's secret. She might also have been afraid for her own life."

Dee nodded. Somehow, though, Mrs. Hughes had found the courage to speak up to tell Detective Hardy that her husband was a murderer.

She had since packed up their house in Wallen and returned to Toronto. Dee had not seen her again after the night of the fire.

Others had left, too.

Vivien was still in the hospital in the city recovering from her chest wounds and would be for a while yet. The family had moved out of the old Martin house to be near her. Dee doubted she'd ever see them again.

And still more were gone.

"Where do you think Podge and his mother went?" Dee turned from the window to her gran. Detective Hardy had made sure that Podge had been released from jail the evening Dr. Hughes was arrested.

"I don't know. Somewhere no one knows them. They have each other. I'm sure they are fine," Gran assured her.

"I think Detective Hardy knew that they would leave. That's why he insisted Podge be let out," Dee said. "If he'd waited, Podge would have had to go into an asylum."

"He's a good man," Gran said.

Dee and the detective had had a long discussion and Dee told him that she thought Podge had come upon Mary Ann shortly after Dr. Hughes had buried her. "I think Podge can naturally *feel* things like I do," she'd said. "I think he felt that Mary Ann was lonely and sad, so he moved her to the spruce tree because she used to be happy there."

Dee felt a pressure on her shoulder and saw that her grandmother had fallen asleep, her head resting on Dee.

Gran had lost a lot of blood from her head wound but had refused to go to the hospital, so Dee, with Cissy's help, had nursed her back to health. Dee worried about her, saw her grandmother's new frailness, then reminded herself that this was Gran, a stubborn woman. She'd be around for a while.

Much to Ray Price's disgust, they were living with Cissy until their house was rebuilt. Dee disliked the smell of smoke, with its sad memories, that still clung to the site, but the men in the village had come together, spurred on by Ray's desire to be rid of her and her grandmother, and started to build them a new home. A new start, Dee told herself.

Dee listened to the train wheels clacking on the rails. So much had changed: her friends, the school, the village, and mostly, Dee herself. Here she was going to see her mama for the very first time. Her stomach fluttered with excitement.

One evening while Gran lay in bed recovering, she had told Dee about her mother. Nothing could have prepared Dee for the surprises revealed that night, the first being that it was Gran, not her mama, who had named the baby girl Defiance.

"I knew you would have a hard life as a motherless and fatherless child. I wanted you to have a strong name to face all those people who would look askance at you."

"But why did you never call me by my name?" Dee asked.

"I made a lot of mistakes," Gran admitted. "And that was one of them. I named you, but I couldn't bring myself to *say* your name. If I did, it would bring back all the horror of that night I found your mother up the mountain . . ." Gran shook her head. "I am sorry."

Gran had then told Dee the story of *feeling* something was wrong with her daughter, a *feeling* so strong, she had gone up the mountain in the dark, only to find her daughter crawling along a path, bleeding and trying to get home.

"For nine months I kept her here with me. I wouldn't let anyone, not even Cissy, come and see her. I was afraid the killer would come back for her if he knew about the baby. Then she had you. You were such a beautiful baby, but not even your birth could bring her mind back from that awful night she'd been attacked. She kept leaving the house late at night while I slept and going up the mountain. I couldn't raise a baby and keep an eye on her, too. So, I did what I thought was best. I put her in the asylum. And then I told everyone she had gone away with a travelling show, thinking to make it easier on you. Every month I visit with her, but she doesn't know who I am. I believe it's a comfort to her, though, to have me there."

"How did we not know it was him?" Dee had asked Gran, as she had questioned herself many times over the last three weeks.

"As I said, evil has a way of disguising itself," Gran said.

"It's gone now," Dee said.

"It's never gone," Gran had told her. "We must be vigilant, but we can't let fear take over our lives. There is a great deal of good in the world. Place your hope on that."

At the train station they hired a carriage to take them to the asylum at the edge of town. Dee stood a moment, heart hammering, staring at the large yellow-stone building, blackened chimneys rising from its roof. She buried her face in the boughs she'd brought and breathed the scent in deeply. It smelled of her mountain. It steadied her.

As they approached, Dee saw bars on the windows.

"It's like a jail," she said, dismayed.

"There are a lot of damaged souls in here. They need to be protected." Gran put her arm through Dee's. "I'll be with you the entire time."

Dee had never been more thankful for her grandmother than at that moment. This woman, who had raised her, loved her, and showed her how to meet life on her own terms, had never once complained that she was raising her grandchild; this woman, Dee realized, she loved deeply. No mother could have done better. Dee squeezed her grandmother's hand, hoping that the gratitude she felt would flow from her into her grandmother. "Thank you," she said.

Inside the asylum, they followed an orderly down a corridor toward her mother's room. Dee's eyes swept around the hall, seeing the patients in nightclothes, empty eyes, shuffling, some yelling to an invisible presence. They were a lost people. "Nurses are needed here, too, Gran," she said.

"It would take a special kind of nurse to do this work."

"Well, I'm not squeamish," Dee told her. "Detective Hardy told me I could stay with him and his wife when I'm in the city for my training."

"You could be a doctor," Gran suggested. "Find ways to heal minds."

"I just might," Dee said.

She had so many plans floating around inside her head, including a visit to a certain village in France.

The attendant stopped at a door and unlocked it. Dee smiled at her grandmother, turned the handle, and opened the door.

"Hello, Mama."

ACKNOWLEDGEMENTS

We travel blithely through life with many people around us, and then one is suddenly taken away. It is only then that we realize how much these people mean to us. Thank you to all my fellow travellers for enriching my life. I hold my friends close to my heart. Many thanks also to my agent, Scott Treimel, and his assistant, John Cusick, who watch out for me, and to my editor, Lynne Missen, who wants only to make my writing better. And last, but never least, thank you to Joe for the long journey together, past, present, and future.